Craig!
Thanks for your help. Hope you enjoy the book.

Gene

SO HARD TO KNOW

Gene Caffrey

So Hard to Know
©2021 by Eugene I. Caffrey

All rights reserved. No part of this publication may be reproduced, distributed, or transmitted in any form or by any means, including photocopying, recording, or other electronic or mechanical methods, without the prior written permission of the publisher, except in the case of brief quotations embodied in critical reviews and certain other noncommercial uses permitted by copyright law.

ISBN: 978-0-9993209-7-6

Automat Catalog #A058
V5.0
0 9 8 7 6 5 4 3 2 1

Published by

Automat.Press
//automat.press
Austin, Texas USA
Design and layout by
¡caliente!design
//caliente.design
Austin, Texas USA

Also by Gene Caffrey:

Shock Treatment
Two Souls
Sweet Caroline
Finding Bridget

PREFACE

There is, in fact, an Innocence Project office in Philadelphia, associated with Temple Universitity Law School. And, in fact, there was a Kensington Strangler who strangled and raped several women in the Kensington neighborhood for two years before being caught in 2011. And further, there was, in fact, a Frankford slasher who, though believed to have been responsible for serial stabbings in the Frankford neighborhood (adjacent to Kensington) in the late 1980s, was charged and convicted on just one of those homicides, the last in the series.

While *So Hard to Know* draws on these facts, it is a work of fiction. The Innocence Project described in the book, though probably somewhat similar to the actual Innocence Project, is a creation of the author's imagination. And Charles Swenson, the alleged Kesington Strangler in the novel, is a fictional character loosely drawn up as a composite of the Frankford Slasher and the Kensington Strangler.

In all other respects *So Hard to Know* is a complete work of fiction and any resemblance of its characters to persons living or decased is unintended and completely co-incidental.

GC

PROLOGUE

South Beach, Friday Before Election Day

When Owen awoke, he was in the dark. Literally and figuratively. There was no light whatsoever. The darkness was thick and oppressive, and his breathing faltered as it always did when claustrophobia began to overwhelm him. He sat up and hunted for his phone but it was not in his pocket. He pawed around the hard grainy floor on which he sat, but couldn't find it. Then he remembered he'd left it in his car somewhere, attached to a wire of some sort. Oh. The charging cord. The effort at remembering that little detail exhausted him enough for his panic to diminish and he eased himself back down onto his back, closing his eyes again.

The next time he woke, he remembered he had no phone but also remembered he could get a little light from his fitbit. He pressed the *on* button. Still woozy, he couldn't read the blurry digits that would have told him the time; but he aimed the light from the fitbit around his cell, or whatever it was. The luminescence was too weak to help. He tried to stand but wobbled and sat down. Then, still fighting his claustrophobia, he lay back and closed his eyes again.

The third time he awoke was more productive. He could read his watch. It was four o'clock, AM he presumed, from the darkness. Though it could as easily be afternoon in a dark basement. He crawled around. The movement relieved some of his panic. He was not buried alive in an oversized coffin. He soon bumped into what felt like strips of plastic fabric connected to metal tubes. Like the floor, they too were gritty. Probably sand. He must still be near the beach. He fingered the metal tubes and concluded they were the frames of beach chairs. That would make sense of the plastic. He must be in some kind of storage shed for the beach chair concession. That would mean he was not in a dark cellar. That would mean it was four AM. He limped his way around the shed, feeling for a door, bumping as he went into what he now immediately recognized as beach umbrellas. He found what he thought was the door and pushed on it; but it was locked from the outside. It flexed some as he put his weight into it; but he did not have enough strength to force it open. He tried to remember if he'd noticed the shed on his walk to the water's edge. He couldn't remember, but guessed it had to be far enough back from the water to be safe in high tides. Maybe close enough to that park for someone to hear him.

Owen's calls for help were feeble. He was weak, the effort was tiring, and he despaired of anyone hearing him. Probably wasn't anyone around at that hour anyway. He plunked himself down on his butt and stared at the hairline of faint light he could now detect outlining the shed door. He put his hand to the pounding ache on the right side of his head and felt what had to be dried blood. Then he laid himself down on his back and fell asleep one more time.

PART I
APACHE TEARS

Chapter 1

Philadelphia. Three weeks earlier . . .

Owen was surprised by the elegance of Glassman's office. The Innocence Project was supposedly a non-profit, scrounging for funds to continue its good work. The older building at the far east end of Market Street, where the Project had recently moved from free space at a city law school, was like the rest of the neighborhood. Nondescript. Sexless. The elevator was creaky, the hallway carpets worn and the walls painted institutional beige and pale green. In the Project's rabbit warren of cubicles, staffers dressed casually—or worse. But Robert Glassman's own digs reminded Owen of the top-tier law firms he had known when his father was alive. A twenty something in jeans had lead Owen to Glassman's open door and said "Bob, Owen Delaney, your ten o'clock," and had then left Owen to fend for himself.

Robert Glassman's appearance was up to the standards of his soothingly painted, lushly papered, deeply polished and oriental carpeted office. Dark, pin-stripped suit. Thick, silver hair. He waved Owen to a leather chair across from his huge rosewood desk and leaned back in his own reclining throne without getting up. Owen sat and was about to begin his rehearsed spiel when Glassman spoke first.

"Owen Delaney. Any relation to my old friend Hank Delaney?"

Owen swallowed. In the nearly eighteen years since his father's fatal heart attack, he had tried to put all memories of the man behind him. But he managed a quiet "Yes, he was my father. Or rather, my stepfather."

"Good man. I knew him when I practiced with Boyd and Mitchell." He waved an open palm as though offering Owen the riches of his posh office. "That's where all this stuff came from. Brought it with me when I took an early retirement. Decided to do something more meaningful with my life. Your dad's—or stepdad's—early passing was actually a motivating factor." He eased his recliner forward and said "So what can I do for you? Okay to call you Owen?"

"Sure." Owen couldn't decide whether to start with his background story—his amateur sleuthing, his detective license and all that—or go directly to his request. He decided to make his ask right off the bat. "Deputy Police Commissioner Kopinski suggested I see if you have any cases that I might be able to work on as a sabbatical project. I teach at the University and I've just begun my sabbatical leave this semester."

"Sabbatical? What do you teach, Owen?"

"Literature. But I worked with the Deputy Commissioner on a few matters while he was a detective."

"And you say Kopinski sent you to me. What was he thinking?"

"Well, I asked if he had any cold cases that I could work on during my sabbatical and he said that the department had its own staff for that. But if I wanted to try what he called 'armchair' detective work, I should ask the Innocence Project."

"'Armchair' detective work. That's an interesting way of putting it; but I guess it's more or less accurate. Most of our staff are volunteers: law students, DNA specialists, that sort of thing. There's no real exposure to violence or danger, if that's what Kopinski was thinking."

"That's it precisely. I've gotten involved in matters that became quite dangerous and I want to avoid all that. My wife had a hard time with it, understandably. But I really do like the detective part. It's a challemging intellectual exercise."

If Glassman hadn't said he'd been a friend of big Hank Delaney, Owen might have tried to explain, without raising an impulse he couldn't quite understand to the level of a virtue, that what he enjoyed as much as the intellectual exercise was righting wrongs, bringing justice to the world. Whatever. But he knew Big Hank would never have understood that and he worried that, despite his current position, Glassman might share some of his stepfather's cynicism. Pausing no more than five seconds to consider and reject the higher-good tack, he went on about the detective part.

"And I think I'm pretty good at it. I even have a state private detective license. And I did go to law school, for what that's worth."

Glassman had apparently not noticed Owen's flash of indecision. "I thought you needed experience in law enforcement to qualify for a private detective license. Were you a cop before you became a teacher?"

"No, the license was arranged by Kopinski as a sort of reward for helping him with a case at the University."

Glassman leaned back again, puckered his lips for a few seconds and then said "Maybe we have something for you. Let me tell you about it and see if you're interested."

For the next ten minutes, Glassman detailed the case of Charles Swenson, convicted of murdering an elderly woman in Kensington way back in 1992. He was now in his sixties. Apparently he had proclaimed innocence all along and, once he learned about the formation of the Philadelphia Innocence Project in 2009, he began writing it monthly letters asking for help.

According to Swenson, all the evidence against him was circumstantial. Glassman was impressed by Swenson's persistence, though not persuaded that his narrative justified taking time away from other cases that offered easier solutions via DNA or retracted eye-witness testimony, particularly since Swenson was also suspected—though never accused or tried—of other murders of elderly women in the area. The Project had never responded to him other than with form letters acknowledging receipt of his request and cautioning that the Project was overwhelmed with such requests and could not promise immediate attention. Glassman gave Owen his file of Swenson letters and said the Swenson matter might be a good start. He suggested that Owen contact Arthur Marx who was DA back at the time of the Swenson trial.

Arthur Marx had retired to Margate at the Jersey shore with two pensions after a long stint in the Philadelphia DA's office and another career as a Common Pleas judge. It took only a few calls to locate him; and Owen was pleased that, on reaching him, Marx was open to discussing the Swenson case, which he remembered quite well.

A few days after his visit to Glassman, Owen found himself cruising Ventnor Avenue in Margate and parking in front of a white stone house near the corner of Ventnor and Quincy. It was one of many stone homes in the area and could have blended nicely into Owen's posh Chestnut Hill neighborhood in Philadelphia. Ventnor appeared to be as much a year round community as a summer getaway.

Marx, seventy-ish, answered the door in khakis and a sweater, holding a pipe. Owen could not remember the last time he had seen anyone smoking a pipe. Marx led him to a den that smelled of sweet tobacco and was filled with the usual photos and memorabilia of a retired pol. They sat at adjacent upholstered armchairs.

"So, the Innocence Project is interested in the Swenson case?"

"Not really. I think they've asked me to look into it just to get Swenson off their back."

"And you say this work is what you want to do for your sabbatical from the University?"

"Yes, at least something like it. My department chair isn't too thrilled about it. I teach Literature; but the rules are that I can work on anything I want. Or even do nothing at all."

"I can imagine your University peers would think it's odd. But tell me, why *do* you want to do this?"

Owen went into an overly long description of his detective "career". Marx smiled as Owen told the stories of his stumbling on to murders that no one knew were committed and his frustrations trying to convince authorities that they had actually occurred. Marx sucked on his pipe and squinted for what seemed to Owen to be a long time. Owen was tempted to break the silence and wax philosophical with the old man about his need, if that was the right word, to see things put right with the world. But he didn't; and when Marx put his pipe down, Owen skipped on to Kopinski and told Marx the Swenson assignment had its origins in a suggestion by him, Marx nodded and said "Okay, that all makes sense; and Kopinski's a good man. I remember him when he was just starting out."

Marx refilled and relit his pipe, puffing on it like an exotic fish, examining the red glow until he was satisfied with its draft.

"So tell me, what do you know about the Swenson case?"

Owen took a deep breath. "Not that much. Just that he was convicted of a fatal, late-night stabbing and robbery of an elderly woman in Kensington, behind a pizza shop as I recall."

"No, it was a dry cleaner's."

"Oh yeah. Dry cleaner's. The guy who identified him—who said he knew him from the neighborhood—said he'd been walking past the pizza . . . dry cleaner's . . . when he saw Swenson standing in front, smoking and talking to an older woman. They all chatted a few minutes and the witness moved on. The eyewitness lived not far from the dry cleaners and told the police about Swenson the next morning when they responded to a call about a dead body in the alley adjacent to the dry cleaners. The dead woman had been at a bingo game that night and won a big pot; but she had no cash on her person. Swenson had no alibi for the evening other than being at a Phillies game alone; and he had a sizeable amount of cash on him when he was picked up the next morning."

Marx pulled his pipe away from his mouth and held it off to the side of his face. "Yes, that's about it for the basics." He pointed his pipe stem at Owen. "But you should also know that we suspected him of prior murders, stranglings and rapes of other elderly women, also in Kensington. And when Swenson was arrested and then incarcerated, those other killings stopped. So we figured we had gotten our man. I think he got life."

"That he did. But he was never tried for those other murders. Isn't that correct?"

"Yes. That was well before DNA tests were perfected. And the Assistant DA working the case said he had nothing concrete to tie Swenson to those other killings. But as I say, the string of killings stopped when he was put away."

"I can see why the Innocence Project isn't all that interested in his case. And I don't know whether it makes any sense for me. Seems like he was probably guilty. Not a good case for someone like me who wants to feel he'd helped justice prevail, if that's not too grand a way of putting it."

"Right, you probably wouldn't find anything. But you never know. All our evidence for the bingo night stabbing was circumstantial. Our office was very aggressive with the case because we suspected he was the serial killer. My lead assistant made a real name for himself when he claimed afterwards that they'd undoubtedly put away the Kensington Strangler. The papers even began to refer to Swenson as the Strangler."

"Who was that assistant?" Owen had a note pad on his lap and pulled a pen from his pocket.

"I'm sure you'll recognize the name. John Ranzone."

"The guy running for governor?"

"Yep." Marx was puffing on his pipe again.

"I wonder if I should talk to him?"

"I doubt he'd give you the time for an interview. Running for office is a hectic job. I remember it well; and I was only running for Philadelphia DA, not governor. And remember, he's serving as DA at the same time." Marks shook his head and exhaled through his nose. "I've always said that Pennsylvania should have a Resign to Run law. But most pols don't like the idea."

"Well, maybe I should drop this Swenson thing and ask for something else."

"I don't know. Try talking to Swenson himself before dropping it. We could have been wrong, you know."

Marx's openness to error was surprising to Owen. From what seemed like dozens of TV interviews with DA's across the country who'd put away killers or rapists later proved to be innocent, he'd assumed that prosecutors never admitted error. It was always puzzling to him why they didn't. They could just acknowledge a mistake, apologize, and act pleased that justice had finally been done. He asked Marx about that.

Marx set his pipe down in an ashtray on the low table between them and leaned back, fingers steepled at his chin.

"As you know, I've been retired for about twenty years from the DA office and might not be so open if I were still in office, particularly if I planned to run again. But more than that, I think it's just natural, after you've put in the prosecutorial work, to believe, actually to *need* to believe, that you were right. Your peers in the DA's office all value convictions. To a large degree, you career depends on them. So when your work is challenged later, you come up with all sorts of rationalizations why the new evidence has flaws. Take recanted witness testimony, for example. I know I was always suspect of that, at least where the witness traveled in the same circles as the doer."

"Why was that?"

"Well, Philadelphia's a city of tight neighborhoods, right? Let's just say a young punk shoots a shopkeeper in his neighborhood during a robbery. Kills him. A neighbor, let's say he was a friend of the victim, maybe even a relative, identifies the punk. Says he's positive he saw him with a gun running out of the shop. The punk is put away for life. After a few years, the punk's friends or family start putting pressure on the witness to recant. They've known the witness themselves for years and still see him in the neighborhood on a regular basis. They argue that the punk has been punished enough. That he's no longer a punk. Time to let him out. Maybe they even offer the witness some money. I'm not suggesting intimidation; just a calming down of hard feelings. The witness agrees to say he really wasn't sure about what he saw and, bingo, the case is opened and the punk goes free. I believe that scenario happened a number of times on my watch. I always thought of it as a kind of street-based commutation of the doer's sentence."

"Okay, I get that. It's possible. But what about DNA evidence?"

"That may be different. But in the days when I was District Attorney, that technology was not well developed. There was no DNA testing in the Swenson case, for example. But I assume some hard-nosed prosecutors have rationalized ways that the new DNA proof is bogus. You'd have to talk to someone younger than me."

Owen wrapped up the conversation, thanked Marx and left, unsure what he would do. But by the time he was on the Atlantic City Expressway headed back to Philadelphia, he decided he should have a little chat with Swenson. See if the conversation pushed any do-gooder buttons.

Chapter 2

John Ranzone checked himself out in the mirror of his suite. He knew the crowd at the breakfast fund-raiser downstairs would be dressed like they were at their local diner. Successful farmers, trucking company owners, All-State insurance brokers, small town bankers. But shirtsleeves and sweaters were not for him unless he was working a county fair or a Penn State tailgate party. No. He wanted to be seen in a suit and tie. Of course, out here the suits were always boxy brown or unsophisticated plaid, with crazily unmatched ties; while in Philadelphia and Pittsburgh the suits were well-tailored, dark blue or grey, with ties of subdued silk.

Half empty Styrofoam cups sat on the coffee table in the seating area, but he was now alone. Before leaving him to think through his speech, everyone on his staff agreed that the speech should be what they called "medium-purple," more blue than red. Speeches for what he thought of as the Pennsylvania "coasts" were easy. Dark Blue. And in the central part of the state, bright red. But in these areas like York, halfway between the extremes, it was an art to tailor his stump speech to the audience. He checked off the main points of his "medium purple". First, happy to be back to an area he's loved since he played ball for Franklin and Marshall college in Lancaster. Met his wife there and came back most holidays with her and the twins and their families to visit her parents and brothers. Dairy farmers. Great people. Parents still going at eighty-seven. The family taught him how to hunt. Always had fresh killed venison for Thanksgiving dinner. Next some explanation for why he went back to Philadelphia. Easy answer. Jobs. Which leads to the next bullet point: protecting the area's jobs and stimulating more opportunity for central Pennsylvania. He toyed with the idea of going more red, skipping the job part and going right to his law and order finale, mentioning his being a former Philly cop as well as current DA. Maybe even use the bit about parts of Philadelphia being like a third world country. But he decided to stick with the staff's suggestions. Even Phil voted for "medium-purple." So he'd hit on jobs and then segue lightly to law and order. He'd promise protection from the vague bogeymen who scared the good people of York and knew he'd bring down the house with his dog whistle mantra: "I know what you want and what the big cities need. And I'll fight for both."

After the breakfast—medium purple was right on—the staff headed west to set up the evening's event in Carlisle; and Phil Conry hustled Ranzone to the York airport for a quick flight to Philly where, at mid-day, he was going to address the Electrical Workers Union. Again. The small Beechcraft turboprop was noisy and Ranzone signaled to Phil that he wanted to get a little shut-eye. He'd have to wake well before they landed to give himself time to struggle into a change of clothes in the narrow aisle of the plane, and he was already tired. He wasn't able to sustain the late nights like he used to. Closing his eyes but unable to fall asleep, his mind raced with pre-election analysis. Live voting was eight days away and the polls were strong. All he had to do was avoid mistakes. Seventh inning, four run lead. He looked at the campaign ahead the way he'd think through the batting order his pitchers would face in the late innings; and saw nothing to worry him. When he looked back, all he could think of was the very unlikely possibility of Calderone bringing up the deal they'd made. Or, equally unlikely, someone raising questions about the Swenson case. Sighing, he finally fell asleep.

Chapter 3

Owen had never been in a prison before and was shocked at its cleanliness. He'd expected a graffiti-covered, Dickensian hovel; but inside, SCI Phoenix prison, built on the grounds of the old Graterford prison, was more like a clean Dutch village. Brightly lit, floors gleaming, everything colorfully painted. A helluva lot better kept up than the offices at the Innocence Project.

Waiting in a subtle yellow reception area for an escort to the meet with Swenson, Owen browsed through the batch of Swenson's letters Glassman had given him. He hadn't read them before and quickly noticed that there were only three distinct texts. All the rest were copies of one of those three. The handwriting was shaky; but the language had a kind of awkward formality that sounded intelligent. He read one at random:

To Whom It May Concern;

> *My name is Charles Swenson. In 1992, at a trial in Philadelphia, I was convicted of a murder I did not commit. I am presently incarcerated at SCI Phoenix prison (formerly Graterford), serving a life sentence.*
>
> *The evidence produced at the aforesaid trial was entirely circumstantial and I believe the public defender assigned to the aforesaid trial was too inexperienced to provide the undersigned with an adequate defense.*
>
> *I respectfully request your assistance in proving my innocence.*
>
> *Mr. Charles Swenson*

He knew Swenson was in his mid sixties. From the letters he expected him to be competent, decently groomed and well spoken, though maybe a little pedantic. But Swenson was not what he expected. Scrawny and pale, with thinning hair, close-bitten fingernails and bad teeth, his hands twitched and he looked pathetic in his oversized coveralls. He could not make eye contact with Owen; and Owen's first impression was that he was sitting across from a guilty man. No question that, if Swenson'd had the same bearing as a forty year old at trial, a jury would make that quick assessment as well.

Owen pulled out the letter he had read in the waiting room.

"Ths letter was pretty well written. Must have taken a long time to work on it."

Swenson had a stutter. "Oh, I did . . . d . . . n't write them letters. B . . . B . . . Bill Donavan who worked in the p . . . p . . . prison liberry wrote 'em. I could n . . . n . . . never write them in a million years. I just c . . . c . . . copied 'em over an over."

One tortuous sentence. But it put a check mark next to Owen's first impression that Swenson would have made a terrible witness for himself at trial.

"You say in your letter that all the evidence presented against you at your trial was circumstantial. From what I know at this point, that's correct. But circumstantial can lead to a correct verdict, you know. Tell me how it was wrong."

Owen tried to quash as unfair his recurring thought that, if Swenson's performance at his trial was anything like his attempt to answer Owen's questions, it was no wonder he was convicted. He stammered, took deep breaths, sweated. Owen wasn't sure whether he should feel sorry for him or angry with him for wasting everyone's time. But, slowly and painfully, with Owen prodding gently, Swenson's version of events came out.

According to Swenson, he had gone, alone, to a Phillies game that night, took the subway from the stadium to Market Street and switched there to the Market/Frankford El which brought him back to the Kensington/Frankford area. He got off at the Tioga street station, which was nearest to where he lived in a tiny room with a small fridge and microwave above a pizza shop on Kensington Avenue. While he was walking south along Kensington Avenue toward home, he did meet Jimmy Phelan, the critical witness in the case. But he insisted that meeting was at least two blocks south on Kensington Avenue from the dry cleaners where the old woman was murdered and where Phelan said he saw Swenson smoking and talking to her. Phelan lived on the Avenue a short distance north of the dry cleaners. So they crossed paths on their ways home: Swenson from the Phillies game and Phelan from Barkley's, a local bar on the Avenue where they all hung out.

At this point, Owen felt some cross-examination was in order. "So what. You and the woman could have walked north, back to the dry cleaners, and you could've killed her there."

"Yeah, if I d . . . d . . . did it. But I n . . . n . . . never saw that wo . . . wo . . . woman. That f . . . f . . . fuckin' DA wo . . . wo . . . wouldn't take my word over a lyin' drunk . . . He was mean. Asked if I always smoked and ch . . . ch . . . chatted up my victims before an attack."

When Owen asked why Phelan would lie, Swenson, with great difficulty, explained that when they met, Phelan asked for money Swenson owed him. Swenson said he didn't have it even though he had been paid that day for a week of grunt work he'd done at a contruction site near Five Points in northeast Philly. Phelan didn't know about the Five Points money and he was pissed that Swenson was short again. Swenson believes he lied about the woman because he was mad.

"How much money did you have on you?"

"'B . . . b . . . 'bout five hundred."

Owen remembered that was the amount of the bingo pot the dead woman had won that night.

"Tell me, Charles, did you ever go to that bingo game. Or know people who did?"

"N . . . n . . . no. But that fuckin' DA made it s . . . s . . . sound like everybody on the Avenue was talkin' b . . . b . . . 'bout it and I must have h . . . h . . . heard. An' I got all excited when I saw her comin'."

Owen sat back in his stiff wooden chair and stared at Swenson. He decided to broach the big question, why the Kensington Strangler murders stopped once he was in custody. The question vitalized Swenson and, almost losing his stutter, he insisted he had nothing to do with those murders and that he was never accused of them. He was sure that, had there been any real evidence to connect him to them, Ranzone, who'd been a bastard throughout the trial, would have gone for broke. Owen decided to let the topic ride until he had decided what to recommend to the Innocence Project.

While Owen had not yet formulated any impression of Swenson's guilt or innocence, he did accept as fact that, without a competent defense, he would have been a pushover for an aggressive DA like Ranzone appeared to have been. He figured a close look at the Swenson's arrest and court files would make sense.

Chapter 4

Glassman didn't think Owen's report justified the Innocence Project's expenditure for the transcripts of Swenson's hearings and trial. So Owen paid for them out of his own pocket. It was hundreds of dollars and, as so often happened when he spent money on what seemed like an extravagance, he had to remind himself that he was a rich man. When the transcripts arrived at the elegant Chestnut Hill home he'd inherited from his mom and Glassman's old friend Hank Delaney, he plunked them on the desk in his spacious office and read every word.

Reviewing these materials was exactly what he had in mind when he conceived of his sabbatical project. Crime solving as an academic exercise, with hopefully a righting of a long buried wrong. He made comprehensive notes on legal sized yellow pads, noting that James Phelan, the state's key witness, denied vehemently that he held a grudge against Swenson, that Swenson never borrowed money from him and that he had no reason to lie about his encounter with Swenson the night of the murder. More incriminating was the testimony of Philip Conry (the lead homicide detective on the case whom Ranzone walked through all the familiar evidence against Swenson at both the trial and the pre-trial hearings). Accordfing to Conry, when Swenson was apprehended he had a knife in his pocket which, though clean, was the size forensics determined the murder weapon to have been. And most damning of all was the testimony of a Greg Stuart, another tenant in the rooming house where Swenson lived. Stuart claimed to have seen Swenson cleaning that knife in their communal bathroom about one a.m. when he himself returned from Barkley's. Also interesting was that there was no mention of the Kensington Stranglings. Pessumably, the judge had stricken them from the record since, otherwise, the Stranglings were the subtext of much of Ranzone's case. At every chance he got, Ranzone had been aggressive to the point of being almost mean. At one point, over failed objections from Swenson's public defender, he even demanded repeatedly that Swenson tell him what chemicals he'd used to clean his knife. Swenson seemed to break under this barrage and Ranzone mocked him as a weakling who picked on old ladies in the night. When Swenson's public defender didn't object, the judge cautioned Ranzone on her own initiative.

Ranzone's summation to the jury was what Owen would have expected: a spelling out of the many coincidences for which Swenson had a weak or no explanation—the eyewitness placing him at the scene at the right time, the money, the knife and its mysterious late night cleaning, the inability to corroborate his Phillies game alibi—and a finish that demanded the jury use their own common sense. Consider the evidence and consider the kind of man they saw before them.

Swenson's public defender, a Peter Martin, on the other hand, was almost timid. While he led Swanson through his story with some clarity, he could not make Swenson believable on the matters that counted. He had no corroboration of the Five Points day labor project and was very unassertive in challenging Jimmy Phelan's testimony about seeing Swenson and the dead woman in front of the dry cleaners at about the time the murder was committed. He did not even cross examine Greg Stuart about the knife cleaning and made no attempt to develop the Phillies game alibi. Reading the transcripts, Owen concluded that, had he been on that jury, he would have voted "guilty."

Chapter 5

Finishing his notes from the trial at about the time the kids returned from school, Owen spent a little time working with Little Hank on his sixth grade math while Claire watched Sesame Street. Little Hank had stopped watching that program well before age nine, and Owen wondered whether that told him something about Little Hank or about Claire who still loved Big Bird at that age. At one point when Hank excused himself for a bathroom visit just as he was struggling with an problem in introductory algebra, Owen crossed his arms and leaned back in his chair, realizing he liked this cold case stuff even if it didn't end with proving Swenson innocent. He realized, that somewhat damning trial transcript notwithstanding, he wanted to keep going. He decided to talk to the players in the drama.

The next morning, once the kids were off to school, Owen sat with Barb at the kitchen table for a second cup of coffee. She attempted to show interest in the Swenson details; but was getting ready for a Community Association meeting at 10:30 and could not give the attention Owen had hoped he'd get. But Owen could tell that the case did not raise the apprehensions in Barb that his real life cases did in the past. Even though she had, over time, become what he'd call an associate detective, the cases always scared her. A history of Owen's foolish exposure to danger was probably adequate justification for that. But free of worries for Barbara and feeling like maybe *he* should take up smoking a pipe, he wandered back to his office and began making calls.

He started with Ranzone. He was not at the DA's office, where it was unlikely he'd take the call anyway. But when he told the smoker-voiced receptionist that he was working with the Innocence Project on the Strangler case, she suggested he call the campaign headquarters. The breathless, young sounding fellow who took the call at campaign headquarters had never heard of the Strangler case but he gave Owen the cell phone number for Phil Conry who apparently acted as gatekeeper for Ranzone the candidate. Repeated attempts to reach Conry all ended in voice mail.

So Owen decided to try Peter Martin, the timid public defender. Apparently he was now in private practice with a small firm that included him as one of the named partners. Martin did take his call; but asked that he schedule an appointment for them to talk. He would be glad to help. Owen set up an appointment for two days hence and went back to his transcript notes for more names.

When Jimmy Phelan, Ranzone's critical witness, had taken the stand, he gave his address on Kensington Avenue and Owen found a listing for a James P. Phelan at that address in the only phone book they kept in the house. Unfortunately the book was about four years old (he and Barb had dropped their landline service about that time in favor of exclusive cell phone use) and the Phelan number in that book was no longer in service. Neither "Information" nor PeopleSearch.com could help. Apparently, the Phelans had gone all cellular as well. Likewise for Greg Stuart who had lived in a room above the same pizza shop as Swenson but, according to *PeopleSearch*, had no active land line and had moved many times. But if *PeopleSearch* was accurate, he still lived at an address on Kensington Avenue. So, with Barb having taken advantage of the beautiful October weather and walked to Germantown Avenue for her meeting, Owen decided to take the minivan and drive to Kensington and knock on the both Phelan's and Greg Stuart's doors. Hopefully, someone would be home at one place or another. Even if not, it would be helpful to see the "scene of the crime" first hand, albeit more than twenty years after the event.

Owen could not remember the last time he'd been to Kensington. Probably back in seventh grade when he took public transportation with Reggie Turner to work together on a school project at Reggie's house. Reggie was a black classmate at Germantown Friends School to which Reggie's parents were sacrificing to send him; and Owen had been too embarrassed to invite Reggie to his impressive stone house in Chestnut Hill. As he recalled, when they bussed to Reggie's house, Kensington was a typical, ethnically mixed working class Philly neighborhood. But from recent features in the Inquirer and Philadelphia Magazine, he knew that gentrification was now well underway in the area. Abandoned industrial buildings were being converted to lofts; and more building permits were issued for projects there than for almost anywhere else in the city. He was curious to see the changes to the Kensington he remembered.

He passed through areas with chunks of new housing and obvious renovations of older structures. He couldn't quite remember where Reggie lived; but he thought it was in one of these rehabbed areas. He hoped that was good for the Turners. He reached Kensington Avenue at East Cambria

Street and drove north. Kensington Avenue and its extension, Frankford Avenue, was unlike any other street in Philadelphia, except maybe west Market Street where the El also ran above the road for a short distance. Sun-blocked by the El, the street had the feel of a 1940s film noir, even on a day so lovely that Barb had decided to walk to her meeting. But it had none of the vitality Owen remembered. And it had certainly not yet benefited from the gentrification going on further out in the neighborhood. The street was littered with trash; and maybe thirty percent of the shops were vacant. Evidence of drug use was rampant. He had read that, despite the urban renewal in the neighborhood, Kensington Avenue was still the heroin capital of Philadelphia. Derelicts lay sleeping in doorways and emaciated young people congregated in the shadows. Traffic was slow with many cars pulling over haphazardly to make drug purchases through their open windows. Few police cars were in sight.

He checked the addresses as he drove north. He passed Barkley's. The bar looked tired but was still open for business. Not too far from there was the pizza shop, now a City drug rehab center, where Swenson and Greg Stuart rented their second floor rooms; and soon he came to the address of the dry cleaners where the bingo lady was found. It was shuttered like its neighbors on both sides. Apparently, its last occupant was a wig shop. A body was curled asleep on a cardboard box in the narrow alley running between the former wig shop and the closed Chinese take-out to its north. That had to be the alley where the bingo lady was murdered. A block or so north was the last address he had for Greg Stuart, which was now an empty lot. So he drove on a couple of blocks to Phelan's address, in an incongruous string of tiny row houses.

The old Phelan residence was boarded-up. But in front of the little house next door, an aging white haired woman with a plump but cherubic Irish face was sweeping the sidewalk. Owen noticed a collection of syringes in the pile of debris she was snapping along. He approached her and stood in her path without speaking. When she looked up, he gave her an innocent "hi" and said he was looking for the Phelan's. Did she know anything about them?

The woman gave him quick head-to-toe sneer and then went back up to the head of crazy blond hair. "I must say, you look like an angel. Hope you not the devil in disguise." She gave a throaty laugh. "That's a good one, huh?"

"Not the devil, mam. Just wanted to talk to Jimmy Phelan. About the Strangler case."

The woman lifted her head, half closed her eyes and sighed. "Not that again."

"What d'ya mean, not again?"

"You a writer?"

"No. Why?"

"Writers been comin' around for years askin' about that case. They stopped when Jimmy died. But I guess you didn't know that."

Owen's heart sank a bit with that news; but he inhaled and said "You knew Jimmy?"

"I was more a friend of Marge, That's his wife."

"Is she still alive?"

"Guess so. Heard she moved to live with their kid in South Philly."

"Boy or girl kid."

"Boy. James. Why does that matter?"

Owen assumed it would easier to track Marge down if she were living with a child named Phelan than a married daughter with a new last name. But he didn't want to alarm the white haired woman with the notion that he'd be hunting Marge down; so he changed the subject.

"Did you live here back when the killing occurred?"

"You mean killings, don't you? That guy Swanson killed, what was it, five other women. Raped them too."

"I guess you know, he was never even charged with those other killings."

"Yeah, I know. But everybody 'round here knows he done 'em. They stopped when they put him away, didn't they? Jimmy said at Barkleys they all had him guilty the day he was arrested."

"Jimmy too, I guess."

"Yep. He knew Swenson. Even lent 'im money once 'n a while. The guys from Barkley's were all Swenson's friends too. But Swenson was the Strangler. No way they would let him get away with that."

"I see." Owen nodded, thanked the woman and started back to his car but turned back and asked if she knew Greg Stuart.

"Sure. Not sure where he's living now; but I'm sure you can find him at Barkley's. Or they'll know where to find 'em."

It was not yet noon and Barkley's was nearly empty but smelled of smoke and stale beer. Owen approached the bartender and asked if he knew Greg Stuart. The bartender wrinkled his face at him and asked why he wanted Greg.

"The Swenson case. I'm doing some work on it."

"Writin' a book on it? The big bad Kensington Strangler case?"

"No. Just need some information for Charles."

"What kind of information. I can tell you all you want to know about Charles. He was a regular when I was just startin' out here."

"That's a long time to be working at one bar, isn't it."

"Maybe. But my name's Pete Barkley. My dad left me this place."

"Oh, well in that case, what can you tell me about Charles?"

"What's to tell? Quiet guy. Stutter. Came in here for his shot and beer just about every night. Most daytimes too. Always borrowin' money. Ran up a tab. But when we heard about him bein' the Strangler, everybody thought he was just the type. Never had no lady friends. Had a kinda mean streak. Didn't surprise nobody."

"Greg Stuart testified at the trial."

"That he did." He exhaled and dropped his gaze while he wiped the bar in front of Owen but said "he's playin cards in the corner if you want to talk to him. The one with the Sixers hat. But they don't like their game interrupted."

Owen slid off his barstool and strolled to the corner table and stood to watch the play. The five older guys at the table ignored him until Greg Stuart pushed his Sixer's cap back and stared at Owen. "What the fuck do you want?"

"I had a few questions about the Swenson case, Greg."

All five of them laughed out loud.

"And what questions might they be, blondie?" Greg's face had gone from amused to annoyed.

Owen felt uncomfortable discussing the matter with the other four around; but sensed Stuart was probably not getting up for a private tete-a-tete. So he said "The knife. You sure you saw him cleaning it? How close were you?"

"How close was I? Damn. He was at the sink and I was takin' a leak. It was everybody's bathroom, remember. If you're here to tell me I might be mistaken, you're wastin' your time." He turned to the old guy on his left. "Your deal, Marvin."

Owen frowned and left.

Chapter 6

No one in the Ranzone entourage said a word as they walked to the van. Of course, John had shaken dozens of hands on the way out, smiled all the way and thanked everybody with whom he could make eye contact. But the rest of the staff remained expressionless, until they had all squeezed their way into the van and whooped it up and high fived each other. The rally had exceeded expectations. The crowd was huge and boisterous. The local Democratic pols on the stage with Johnny were beaming and a reporter from the Erie Times News told Phil that Ranzone's poll numbers in the area were better than any Democrat since LBJ. It was almost painful for them all to have to turn their minds to the next day when the campaign moved to Altoona.

In Ranzone's hotel room that night, Phil Conry went over his notes while Ranzone showered and got ready for bed. The next day's schedule in Altoona was packed and John also had to make a few conference calls with the office in Philadelphia. On top of that the mayor wanted him to make a statement about the decreasing crime rate in the city; and several candidates for state representatives were asking for money from his swelling campaign war chest. They also had to carve out some time to prepare for the upcoming debate. When John sloughed out of the bathroom, he sagged onto his bed for Conry's presentation and, exhausted, quickly agreed on the coming agenda. Conry then took out his phone to see if there was anything in his texts or emails that he'd missed.

"Oh, yeah. A guy from the Innocence Project has been leaving messages asking to talk to you about the Kensington Strangler case. What should I tell him?"

"Damn. Tell him we're too busy to go into ancient history. Tell him the case speaks for itself. The jury took less than three hours to convict Swenson. And those Kensington Stranglings stopped as soon as we took him in." Ranzone sighed. "What more does he need to know? Tell 'em to fuck off."

Conry chuckled and pantomimed writing on his pad, mumbling to himself as he did:

"John says to fuck off." He smiled at Ranzone and left for his own room. But Ranzone flopped back onto his bed and stared at the ceiling, his stomach so tight he could barely breathe.

Chapter 7

The day after Owen's trip to Kensington, he took the Chestnut Hill Local to the Market East Station and walked a few blocks to Peter Martin's offices on Walnut Street. Though not particularly impressive, they were a step up from the Innocence Project. From the layout, Owen guessed that the receptionist/paralegal in the small lobby was the only staff other than the two lawyers whose names appeared on the door. She was expecting Owen and asked him to wait in the conference room. The conference room/library was cluttered: dining room sized walnut table stacked with court documents, a few faux-leather captain's chairs, copy machine and a free-standing metal cabinet for supplies. Owen sat and waited.

It took almost five minutes before a shirt sleeved Peter Martin rushed in.

"Sorry, Mr. Delaney. Couldn't get off the phone."

Martin was about fifty, which would have put him in his mid-twenties when he represented Swenson. The waist of his pants was a little tight and his shirt not too neatly pressed. Loosened tie. The lenses of his eyeglasses were smudged, his thinning hair was combed over in-artfully, and his eyes were baggy.

"So you want to talk about the Swenson case? I'm a little ambivalent that the Innocence Project is interested in the case. I guess it could be good for Swenson; but I'd almost prefer that the whole thing was forgotten. I can't say I'm too proud of my work on it."

"I read the transcripts. You seemed... I guess the word is 'inexperienced'."

"Oh, was I. The public defender's office was very short handed at the time; and I was the unlucky newbie drafted to do the job. The two other guys who might have been able to take it came up with some clever excuses. None of them wanted to defend the Kensington Strangler. Might hurt when they went into private practice. Though I was only two years out of law school and had never handled a murder trial, I was an idealistic kid and didn't fight the assignment."

"But, as I understand it, he wasn't being tried as the Strangler."

"Well, not officially. And the judge was sensible enough to sustain all my motions to strike references to the stranglings. But the whole city knew what the case was about."

"And what do you think you should have done better? Do you think Swenson was innocent?"

"No. If I thought he was innocent, I might've have petitioned the court to re-try the case on the grounds that I *was* incompetent. But I didn't know what to think other than I had given it my best effort. The problem was my effort was not up to the standards I'd expect of myself today."

"How so?"

"Well for one, I should never have put him on the stand. I knew he was a fragile sort of guy and Ranzone made mincemeat of him. Thank God the judge took a little pity on him. Or maybe on me. She made a decent attempt to control Ranzone." Martin took off his glasses, noticed the smudges and pinched them clean with his tie before continuing. "And I have to admit my cross examination of that key witness was weak."

"James Phelan?"

"Yup, that was his name. His story was too pat and he was too smooth. Swenson said they'd had a kind of falling out but I couldn't get Phelan to admit it. And I didn't look for others who knew them both who might corroborate Swenson's version. If I had raised even a little doubt about his credibility, the jury might not've been so quick to convict. I don't think they took more than a couple of hours."

"And what about Swenson's other alibis: the Phillies game, the money from that work in Five Points?"

Martin exhaled mightily and shook his head. "I couldn't think of any way to prove he'd been at that game. And even if he was at the game, he still could've been on Kensington Avenue at the time of the murder." He exhaled again. "I did find the contractor who was hiring men from Kensington for that Five Points project but he was uncooperative. Paying them under the table and what not. Said he couldn't remember any one in particular. And Swenson didn't know any of the other guys who were on the job. Said they all heard about it on the street and showed up each morning at K & A. That's the corner of Kensington and Alleghany avenues, in case you don't know. I went there one morning but the corner was empty. No jobs that day, I guess."

"And the guy who said he'd seen Swenson cleaning his knife?"

"I didn't want to touch that. Swenson at first told me the guy was lying; then he told me he cleaned it every night. I couldn't get a straight story from him so I let it go. Probably another mistake."

The conversation with Martin went on for about ten more minutes. When it was finished, Owen found himself hoping that Martin was truly unsure of Swenson's guilt or innocence. It would be hard to live with yourself if you believed the jury had convicted an innocent man because of your inexperience. But perhaps, like the winning DAs who can't admit anyone they convicted was innocent, *losing* defense attorneys can't accept that their convicted clients were innocent either.

On the train back to Chestnut Hill, Owen's cell phone rang. It was Phil Conry, for Ranzone.

"Got your messages, Delaney. And all I can say is that Mr. Ranzone is way too busy to spend time on a decades old case. He says there's no chance that guy Swensom wasn't guilty and the Strangler to boot. As you should know, the stranglings stopped when Swenson was arrested. And the jury took only a couple hours to convict him. John says . . . don't waste your time."

"But what about you? You were the lead detective, weren't you?"

"Yeah, But I got my own hands full with this campaign. The answer's 'maybe later' for me. Sorry, buddy."

Conry hung up and Owen leaned against the window, staring at the familiar decay of north Philadelphia, wondering if gentrification would ever reverse it, and trying to stay positive that this Swenson business was really worth his time. Maybe he should ask Glassman for something else.

Chapter 8

Owen's train got him home before two and he spent some time in his office organizing journal articles he'd read for his last semester's teaching and filing away notes for some planned journal articles of his own. He was sitting at his desk when the kids' school bus pulled up at the end of their long driveway. Hank and Claire were old enough now to make their own way to the back door of the house and let themselves in. But both Owen and Barb dropped what they were doing to meet the kids as they skipped up the driveway. Owen loved being home when they got back from school. Particularly so because they were taking the same school bus from Germantown Friends that he had taken decades before. This sabbatical life and the low stress work he was doing for the Innocence Project really agreed with him.

After sitting with the kids at the round oak kitchen table for snacks, Barb took Claire into the family room to help her prepare for her spelling test the next day and Owen went with Little Hank to his office to work some more on his new math. When they were all finished, they let the kids turn on the TV, Owen and Barb in the kitchen with their eyes on the kids' probable battles over the shows to watch. As Hank flipped through the channels, Owen noticed a promo for a seven o'clock political special that evening on the lives and careers of the candidates in the gubernatorial race. He interrupted the kids' mini-debate, took the remote from Hank, and set the TV to record the special.

When finished with dinner and the usual bedtime fiascos—Barb's little battle with Claire over what she would wear the next day and Hank's panic that he forgot to write a paragraph about some Roman god—Owen and Barb sat in the family room to watch the recorded news and that political special, which apparently was a coming attraction for the gubernatorial debate at Owen's university to be televised the following night. Owen was not an avid follower of politics, but he had developed a curiosity about Ranzone and knew little about him.

The first fifteen minutes of the program was about Ted Wright, the Republican, a businessman from Harrisburg with a typical Republican platform. Less government, lower taxes. All that. Owen was not interested and fast-forwarded to the segment on Ranzone.

The Ranzone piece began with a series of photos and an unseen narrator. The first picture was of a pudgy two year-old in red striped Phillies PJs. According to the voice over, John Fitzgerald Ranzone was born in 1956 and raised in the Olney section of Philadelphia. His mother, Claudia Shanahan Ranzone, a staunch Irish Catholic (flash picture of pretty freckled faced twenty year old), had been an early fan of the handsome Irish Catholic congressman from Massachusetts and insisted on naming her firstborn John Fitzgerald. Her husband, Robert, was a Philadelphia cop (formal portrait in policeman's uniform and cap), and when he passed his detective's exam in 1959, he and Claudia decided to have more children. Three were born in relatively quick succession: Alice, Bill and Douglas (series of family shots, all handsome kids except Douglas who had an awkwardly shaped face. John still pudgy).

As the oldest, John was the leader of the brood and, always big for his age, a standout athlete as a boy (pictures of young John in football gear, basketball shorts and a little league baseball uniform). But by the time he got to high school, he'd decided to concentrate on baseball, making all Catholic as a catcher in his senior year (picture of John in a catcher's crouch, shin guards and chest protector but no headgear), and receiving a baseball scholarship to the small Franklin and Marshall college in Lancater. It was in Lancaster that John met his future wife, Elizabeth Collins (wedding picture, Elizabeth tall and blonde) whom he brought back to Philadelphia where he joined the police force like his dad (picture of John at gradation from police academy). Within a few years, John and Elizabeth had twin girls (series of family shots), and John had passed his detective's exam. After a few years as a detective, John juggled law school with his police work and was awarded his law degree in 1986 (picture of John in cap and gown).

John's first and only legal job was with the Philadelphia District Attorney's office where he began immediately after law school graduation as one of many assistants and continues to this day as the District Attorney himself (series of pictures of a progressively older but also progressively more rotund looking John in suit and tie).

As an assistant DA, John handled many important criminal cases including the infamous Kennsington Strangler case (pictures of newspaper headline about the case, "Strangler Strikes Again in Kensington", etc) and many prosecutions of local politicians for corruption of one sort or another (more pictures of newspaper headlines).

John ran for DA eight years ago as a Democrat and won (picture of wife and twins and grandkids showered with confetti at victory party) and was reelected four years later. While he is term limited and can not run again, he decided to remain in office even while he campaigns for governor (picture of John addressing a big crowd in some outdoor venue).

Excerpts from John's campaign speeches came next. John's policy positions were clear but unorthodox. His law and order positions came natural to him as a former cop and long time DA. But alhough he'd been in law enforcement for many years, he could not adopt the common law-enforcer's endorsement of gun control. Indeed, as an avid hunter, he was opposed to gun control. And his fondness for the heartland of Pennsylvania seemed genuine. He was believable when he said that, though he didn't generally endorse big government spending programs, he thought more money should be spent to develop opportunities out there, even if it meant locating new state offices in more rural areas. He said nothing about abortion except that, as Catholics, he and his wife could never consider it.

When the program ended, Owen said to Barbara "I think I'll go to that debate tomorrow night. See what he feels like in person."

Chapter 9

The debate was held in a mid-sized auditorium at the University and, at the last minute, Owen was able to wangle a ticket from a friend in the political science department. He arrived early and took his assigned seat on the center aisle, about twenty rows back, and watched as the dignitaries and persons he assumed to be family of the candidates were escorted to seats in the front two rows. The mayor was there as well as several congressman he recognized.

Maybe ten minutes before the debate was scheduled to begin, the candidates entered from side doors at the front of the room and glad-handed the dignitaries, smiling and nodding as they accepted what Owen guessed were their good luck wishes. Then both candidates stopped for hugs and kisses with the persons Owen assumed were family. Owen was not particularly interested in Wright's family; but he paid close attention to the group surrounding Ranzone. There was a tall light haired woman who was maybe a young looking sixty-five with two dark haired women in their forties, two college aged girls and one similar aged boy. Owen pegged them as the wife, Elizabeth, the twin girls and three grandchildren. There were also two men and one woman, also sixtyish. One of the men wore clerical garb. Owen guessed they were the Ranzone siblings, Alice, Bill and Doug, if he remembered the names correctly. After the hugs and kisses, Ranzone left the floor, turning at the steps to the stage and blowing redundant, last minute kisses to the people he had just hugged and kissed.

The debate itself was like every other debate Owen had watched on television. And as he did during those debates, he found himself almost nodding off during the wonkish parts and deliberately ignoring the occasional obligatory acrimony. When the debate ended, the moderator thanked the candidates and the audience and the University for providing the venue. The audience gave vigorous applause. Owen had to admit that, as debates go, it was remarkably civil and that he had found Ranzone's style appealing. Though he could most charitably be described as hefty, he had a lightness on his feet as he moved around his podium and an energy Owen found attractive. He seemed much younger than mid sixties as he bounded down the steps from the stage when the applause ended, to mix with his family and political friends.

Owen had gotten up from his seat to let others file out of their row but remained standing in the aisle, studying Ranzone. On a vague impulse, Owen pushed himself down the aisle to the knot of people congregating around Ranzone. By the time he'd wedged himself to three layers back from the candidate, he realized that saying anything to Ranzone about the Swenson case would be as welcome as a protestor at a city council meeting. And much less appropriate. Feeling stupid, Owen started to turn back up the aisle when he heard his name called.

"Professor Delaney! Professor Delaney"! The voice was coming from one of the college aged girls he assumed was a Ranzone grandchild. He recognized her face and was trying to place it when she broke out of the knot surrounding her grandfather, extended her hand and said "Professor Delaney! Remember me? Carol Dames? Your afternoon survey of lit course? Last two semesters?"

Owen did remember. Miss Dames was one of the really bright ones. He had enjoyed having her in class. He'd guess he gave her an 'A'.

"Oh yes. I remember you well. You were a pleasure to have in class." He wasn't sure what else to say under the circumstances. He wasn't going to ask her about Thomas Hardy or Walt Whitman. But he did shake her outstretched hand. She held on to him and pulled him toward the crowd. "Come, let me introduce you to my family," she said.

Ranzone was moving on by then and Owen got only a quick glimpse of his face. On stage, handsome in a pudgy sort of way and made up for the cameras, he looked great for a sixty-five year old. But up close the rigors of the campaign showed. He looked tired. While Owen studied him, the rest of the family group turned toward Owen as Miss Dames towed him into their circle.

"Mom, this is the Professor Delaney I talked about so much."

The mother, the more attractive of the twins, extended a hand, said something pleasant and then introduced Owen to the other family members standing about. Owen's guesses about the family members were right on, except that one of the older men Owen had assumed was Ranzone's brother, Doug, turned out to be Alice's husband, Paul. No Doug in sight.

When Alice extended her hand to him, Owen noticed her glance at his hair. It was often a focus of conversation with new acquaintances, although frequently the conversation didn't immediately start with hair. Many people, struck by its unusual bright silkiness, wanted to touch it or at least talk about it but were uncomfortable doing so. So they would ask him about himself hoping to get around to the hair eventually. Alice appeared to be such a person.

"Are you a political junky, Professor?"

"No, I'm not; but I've been curious about your brother."

"Oh? Why's that?"

"Well, I've been working with the Innocence Project on a case that your brother prosecuted many years ago and, I guess I just wanted to see him in person."

"What case was that, Professor?"

"The Charles Swenson case, 1992."

"Wow, that is a long time ago. I don't remember it. What was it about? Why is the Innocence Project interested?"

"Well, it was a murder case. A Kensington man was convicted of stabbing an older woman. He still says he didn't do it."

"Oh, you mean the Kensington Strangler case? Is that the one?"

"That's what they call the case now; but our client maintains he wasn't the Strangler either. And he was never charged with the stranglings."

"I do remember that case. John was in a frenzy over it. He had always been an easy-going charmer. But not that time. He was out for blood and he was hard to be around. Thank God, he's come off that jag and mellowed."

"Yes. I read the transcripts and find it hard to jibe that young prosecutor with the guy on the stage tonight."

"I agree. But I always thought that frenzy had to do with our mother's death. She was John's biggest fan. She died of cancer right around the time that Swenson guy was arrested. And she was about the same age as the murdered woman. I think John was taking out his grief on Swenson."

"That's an interesting theory. What else can you tell me about that time?"

Just then Alice's husband approached them and touched Alice's arm saying "we should really get going, Allie."

"Right." She turned from Paul to Owen. "If you want to talk more about it, it would probably be best to talk to Father Bill, our brother. He's the family psychologist. He's a monsignor now, but we still call him Father Bill. He's left already but you can reach him at St Francis in University City."

Chapter 10

Owen had been excited by Alice's grief-frenzy theory about Ranzone's aggressiveness toward Swenson when he returned from the debate and talked about it with Barbara. But by morning he wasn't so sure it helped Swanson in any way. So what if Swanson was convicted by an angry, grief-stricken prosecutor and defended by a hapless, inexperienced public defender. If he was guilty, he was guilty, no matter the cast of characters. So, after he saw the kids off on their bus, he went to his desk and logged on to PeopleSearch.com to try to find Marge Phelan, who might actually be able to give Swenson's case a lift if she knew about her husband's supposed spat with Swenson.

There were quite a few Marge Phelans in Philadelphia. Her old neighbor in Kensington had said she's moved in with her son James to South Philly. So he checked James Phelans as well. To his surprise, there were ten results that showed both a Marge and a James Phelan at the same address and the appropriate mother/son ages. If he knew which sections of the city those Swenson addresses were located, he could narrow down the list to those in or near South Philly. So he printed out the list and called up a map of Philadelphia.

After an hour of painstaking search, he came up with three possibles. He made calls to them all. The first one was not answered; but the next two did and denied that the Marge in their household had ever lived in Kensington. That meant the best bet was the first address on the list. Daley Street, not too far from Oregon Avenue.

Anxious to do something, he was reluctant to wait till he reached someone at the Daley Street house. Old Marge had probably gone out for a while, maybe for about the time it would take him to drive down to Daley Street. Or she might actually be there and had one of those landlines with caller ID, but wouldn't answer the phone because she didn't recognize the number. If Barb were not out with the van, he'd drive down to Daley Street and wait at the Phelan house until someone appeared. Though, in theory he could take public transportation to South Philly—take the 23 bus on Germantown, change at 11th and Market for a bus to South Philly and then walk maybe seven or eight blocks—that seemed like a lot of work. And what was he going to do when he got there if no one was home? Sit on the curb and wait?

He decided to rent a car. Barb wouldn't be back for hours but she would certainly be back in plenty of time to meet the kids' bus after school. He knew there was a rental agency nearby that delivered rentals to your home. So he decided to have a rental delivered, drive to Daley Street and wait all day if that's what it took.

While waiting for the rental to be delivered, he looked up St. Francis church in University City where Father Bill Ranzone was stationed. It was not far out of his way on the drive to or from Daley Street. He called the rectory at St. Francis and talked to the housekeeper who fetched the monsignor.

"Morning. Monsignor Ranzone speaking."

"Good morning, monsignor. My name is Owen Delaney. I was at the debate last night and spoke a bit to your sister. She suggested I call you with with some questions I had. She called you the family psychologist."

"Well, maybe I am. But what kind of questions have you got and why will you be asking them?"

"My questions have nothing to do with the campaign, Or politics. Truth is, I'm fishing for information about an old case your brother prosecuted." Owen decided to save time and call it the Kensington Strangler case, which Father Bill immediately remembered. "I'm working with the Innocence Project trying to evaluate Charles Swenson's claims to innocence. Your sister said that your brother was in an unusually intense mood during that trial. She thought it had to do with your mother's death. We didn't get a chance to go very deeply into her ideas; and I'm not sure it makes any difference to Mr. Swenson whether or not your brother was in what Alice called a 'frenzy', but I'd like to get a feel for the psychological dynamics at work at the trial. I've read the transcripts and it does seem that your brother was unusually harsh, maybe even to the point of unfairness to Mr. Swenson."

Father Bill didn't respond for a few seconds. Finally he said "I know the Innocence Project and I respect its work, And, for what it's worth, Alice is right. John was very upset after our mother's death. I'm not sure I'd call it a frenzy; but we all thought he was taking things out on that man Swenson. From what I remember, he was widely believed to be the Kensington Strangler even though he was never tried for those murders. But I suppose it's possible that he wasn't responsible for the murder John prosecuted him for." The monsignor went silent again for a while, then went on. "Interesting moral dilemma for the Innocence Project, isn't it? Man gets away with several murders but is convicted of one he didn't commit. Is that just?"

"Yes. But you understand I'm interested only in the murder for which he was actually convicted."

"Of course. As I said, I know all about the Innocence Project. And I think you deserve more time than I'm able to give right now. I teach some religion classes in the grade school here. So many lay teachers now that our Catholic parents feel shortchanged. But I'll be available about three if that's convenient for you." Owen said yes, hoping he could speak to Marge Phelan beforehand. If not. He'd at least get something for the rental car fee.

Shortly after Owen finished with Father Bill, two cars from the rental agency pulled into the parking area off his driveway. He grabbed his notes, locked up the house as he went out to sign the paperwork, got into his rental and followed the other car out to the street. It turned right and, setting his GPS for the Daley Street address, Owen turned left for South Philadelphia.

Chapter 11

Daley Street was only two blocks long, and very narrow. So narrow that Owen had to park around the corner and walk to the Phelan address. The sidewalks too were narrow, no more than five feet from the house fronts to the curb. But the tiny row houses on both sides of the street each had a different façade, giving the place a continental feel.

From the sidewalk, without balancing himself on the one step stoop, Owen rang the bell to the Phelans and waited. No answer. He clicked his ring on the small pane glass window at the top of the door and waited a little longer until he saw the curtain inside the window move a few inches. A sliver of a worn, pale, female face looked down at him with her eyes fixed on his hair which, from a lifetime of experience, he knew was a good sign.

"Marge Phelan?"

The door remained closed; but he could hear a voice, almost masculine, say "Wha'dya want?"

"I'm looking for Marge Phelan. I have some questions about her husband, Jim."

"Go ahead" the husky voice said. "I'm lisnin."

"It's about the Kensington Strangler case. I'm working with the Innocence Project on the case."

"The what?"

"The Innocence Project. We check out the claims of persons who say they didn't commit the crime they've been convicted of."

"Uh huh."

"Your husband testified against a man named Charles Swenson who was convicted of murdering a Kensington woman, a lady going home from her bingo game."

"Yeah, I remember. People all knew he done the stranglings even though he wern't charged with them."

"That's correct, Mrs. Phelan. But all I'm interested in is whether or not Charles Swenson owed your husband money at the time that woman was killed."

"Why d'ya want to know that?" Mrs. Phelan spoke more quietly and, with the door still closed, Owen had a hard time hearing her. Stupidly, like some a Saturday Night Live character in a conversation with a cabbie who spoke little English, he raised his own voice.

"It could be important for Mr. Swenson."

"You don't have ta scream," she said, but to Owen's relief, she resumed a more normal tone. "Don't see how that could be important. But truth is, that guy Swenson always owed money to Jimmy. I tol' Jim he was stupid to keep lendin' Charles money but, no sooner'n Charles'id pay 'em back, he'd borrow money again. Charles was a real dead beat."

"So you think Charles owed him money at about the time that bingo lady was killed?"

"Prob'ly."

"Did you tell that to the Swenson's lawyer?"

"Nope. Nobody ever talked to me about it."

Owen left Daley Street with a skip in his step, thinking he'd finally peeled away a little skin from the onion. But he had almost two hours before his scheduled meeting with Father Bill and wasn't sure how to make that time go by with the speed his impatience demanded. He decided to get something to eat; and for reasons he could not explain to himself, he thought he'd check to see if any of those pizza places on Snyder Avenue from which he'd staked out the South Philadelphia Social Club many years before were still there.

After a little wandering around, he found the right block. One of the pizza shops was still there—right across the street from the Social Club which had the same solid wood door and black lettering he remembered. He parked near a fire hydrant, (reluctantly, but it was the only space available), and went in. Hunched at a Formica table near the window waiting for his order, he found his thoughts drifting to the events of his first "case", in which that Social Club played a critical role. The memories were bittersweet. Bitter because they included being kidnapped and threatened with violent death. Sweet because he had met Barbara at that time and, to be honest, also because that adventure had roused him from a deep funk and given him a taste for sleuthing and righting wrongs which he realized made him feel more alive and more filled with purpose. He called Barb.

"Hey, Barb. Never guess where I am."

"I give up. Where?"

"Sitting across from the South Philly Social Club."

He thought he heard Barb gasp; and quickly realized that she probably didn't associate that place with meeting him or with any other sweet events in their lives. It was just a link to a horrible episode during which he had risked his life. So he blurted out, "Just stopped for a couple slices of pizza. I rented a car to visit with some people about the Swenson case. One was down here in South Philly."

They talked for a while about their schedules for the day. Barbara was relaxed and, once again, Owen was happy he had thought of this cold case idea. It really suited him, sleuthing without the danger. He knew he didn't have to worry about being kidnapped by old Mrs. Phelan or Father Bill.

Despite spending forever on his pizza and driving like an eighty-year old to St. Francis church, he was still fifteen minutes early for his meeting with Father Bill. Rather than wait in his car, he rang the rectory bell, and introduced himself to the finicky, nun-like housekeeper who opened the door and then escorted him to a dark paneled library off the center hall. At precisely three, Father Bill entered. He had the handsome Ranzone face of Alice and John, but less full. He extended a disturbingly soft hand, said all the usual things and sat down in one of the three upholstered armchairs in the quiet room.

"So, Owen, if I may call you that, what is it you'd like to know?"

Owen explained that he hoped the back-story of Mrs. Ranzone death at the time of the bingo lady slaying might not only explain John Ranzone's aggressive tone, but more importantly, help bolster the case that Swenson's public defender was an inadequate match for such a skilled and angry prosecutor. Owen reported the apparent lie by Jim Phelan he'd uncovered in his conversation with his widow that very morning.

"As they say in Latin, Father, ' falsus in uno, falsus in omnibus', lie in one thing, lie in everything. What else did Phelan lie about? According to the widow, the public defender had never questioned her. Sounds like a rookie mistake."

"So you think Swenson had an inadequate defense and that inadequacy was exacerbated by John's state of mind at the time, that he was too emotionally distraught to be fair."

"Exactly, Father."

Father Bill gave his chin a few slow, thoughtful strokes and said "I guess your request makes sense. If it wasn't so hard to reach John during this campaign, I'd call him first. But I really don't see any harm in giving you the back-story, as you call it."

It took a full forty-five minutes for Father Bill to give the details he thought were important for Owen to understand all that happened. He actually began with their childhood, during which John was a "wonderful big brother." He protected Alice and him at the playground where they all hung out and he doted on little Doug who was what he described as developmentally delayed. John had also been a great example of brotherly love for Doug as they got older. Doug was batboy for all of John's baseball teams and he was allowed to tag along with John just about everywhere. John even invited him for weekend visits at college. Father Bill said he couldn't even remember all the nice things John did.

While Doug managed to graduate from their Catholic high school, it was probably only because the school felt they owed something to the family. John had been an all-Catholic ballplayer, Alice president of the student council and he, Father Bill, to the joy of his old teachers, was already at St. Charles Borromeo seminary when Doug hit the wall academically in about tenth grade.

At that point, Father Bill took a deep breath, then continued. "Doug was about twenty two when our father retired and he and our mother moved to a fifty and older community down the shore. John convinced them to let Doug have the Olney house. He and Alice were both married and settled by then, and I was almost ready to be ordained; but Doug really had no prospects. He did manage to get by with part time jobs here and there, but I'm pretty sure John gave him regular financial help. Neither Alice nor I had any funds to spare, but like John, we would look in on Dougie as frequently as we could,"

Apparently, over time their visits to the Olney house, John's included, became less frequent, although Father Bill was sure John kept up his financial support. He was a busy family man and had little time for those Dougie check-ups. It eventually got to the point where the siblings saw Doug mainly at holidays and family gatherings.

Father Bill paused and shifted in his seat. He made a funny movement with his mouth that looked like he was biting his tongue. Then he exhaled and went on with the story.

"When my mother got cancer about 1990, we were all surprised that Doug made little attempt to visit her. Of course she lived down the shore and Doug had no car. But still, it bothered us. Personally, I put it down to the fact that mom had always been a little ashamed of Doug and he sensed it.

He was a funny looking baby where, in our pictures at least, the rest of us were Gerber baby cute. As he grew into early childhood he showed some physical anomalies. His ears were low set and pointed, he had huge gaps between his toes and his hair was extremely thin and gave off static. Our pediatrician said those things were unimportant but Dad said mom suspected they were birth defects caused by a viral infection during her pregnancy. Whatever the cause, she worried about Douglas from day one. It wouldn't surprise me if he thought she didn't love him. Or at least love him as much as her other children. He may have been right.

"When she died, we decided to have the funeral in Olney so more of her old friends could make it: St. Helena's, that's at Fifth and Godfrey, and a lunch at the Knights of Columbus hall afterwards. Usual Irish wake. But Doug never showed and John was mad about it. He insisted I go with him to the house and confront Dougie. He was so upset, I guess he didn't trust himself. When we got there, there was no answer. John always had a key so we let ourselves in."

Father Bill looked down at his shoes and shook his head, then went on to describe the hovel Doug had been living in. Trash and unfinished TV dinners all over the kitchen, dozens of empty beer cans in the living room. Dirt and grime. He remembered feeling ashamed of himself for letting Doug slide. And he assumed John felt the same way. They went upstairs, thinking Doug might be sleeping off a hangover or worse, but he was not in his room. What was in his room only added to their upset. More beer cans, empty pizza boxes. And an unbelievable collection of graphic pornographic magazines.

"Two of his dresser draws were open and John noticed that they were stuffed with women's nylon stockings. My first thought was that Doug had a girlfriend, which pleased me some. But John understood why Dougie kept those magazines and stockings.

"I think the image of poor Dougie, with no life in that house other than drinking and masturbating, hit John very hard. He grabbed an old baseball bat he'd given Doug that was standing in a corner. I think John gave Doug the bat after hitting three home runs with it in the City championship game. Then he took the bat and gave a wild swing at the stuff on Dougie's dresser. I think he was taking aim at Dougie's huge jar of Apache Tears."

Owen had no idea what Apache Tears were and Father Bill explained that they were rough gemstones that Doug had found out west on a family road trip to Arizona. The stones supposedly were created when a band of Apache woman who had lost their husbands in battle let their tears drop to the dry, barren ground at their feet. Apparently Doug had been proud of his collection even though their mom had harped on him to get rid of them for years. Even threatened to throw them out herself.

"They had lots of fights over them that I could never understand back then. But I now see them as symbolic battles about Doug's feeling unloved by her and her maybe actually disliking him. Whatever they were about, he never threw the stones away."

With the Apache Tears scattered all over Doug's bedroom, John and Father Bill went back downstairs just in time to meet Doug coming in the front door. John could not speak and Father Bill asked where he'd been during the funeral. Doug cried and said he couldn't go because he'd done bad things that she wouldn't like. At that point, John told Father Bill to teach Dougie about what's a sin and what's just part of being human. He stormed out of the house and let Father Bill handle Doug who was devastated by John's anger. Father Bill brought Doug to live at his rectory in North Wales for a few weeks during which Doug blamed his drinking on friends from the neighborhood whom he couldn't shake. Hearing this, John arranged to sell the house and have Doug move to south Florida where John had some college friends who could keep an eye on him. He felt he'd failed Doug and his mom but, already a busy DA and a family man, he was afraid he couldn't put in the time.

"So, Doug lives in Florida?" Owen asked.

"Yes, at least we think so. John's friends couldn't straighten Doug out and his drinking got worse. He moved around a lot and no one in the family has seen him in years. He did call John every once in a while for five years or so, but didn't ever tell him where he was living."

"Hmm. Sad story. Had to be an upsetting time for you all, particularly John."

"Yes. Particularly John. That's why I think the story may have relevance to what you're trying to do for that fellow Swenson. John was not himself for a long while. I don't think I've ever seen him as upset as when he smashed that jar. He was—and he still is—generally a very mild mannered person."

Owen thanked Father Bill, got up from his seat, thanked him again as Father Bill walked him to the door, and thanked him one last time when he turned to wave at the good father as he got into his rental car.

Chapter 12

Phil Conry was in the front seat with their driver. Ranzone was in the back reviewing his notes for the evening event in Williamsport.

"Phil, how do I pronounce the name of the mayor? Is it 'Gah-briel' or 'Gay-briel'?"

"It's Gah-briel but everybody calls him Gabe. You might want to try that too."

The late October days were getting shorter and most cars on the Interstate had their lights on, even at five—thirty. They drove on in silence. Ranzone had just slid his notes onto the seat beside him and closed his eyes when Phil's phone rang. After identifying the caller, Phil leaned over his seat and extended his phone to Ranzone.

"It's your brother. . . . Father Bill."

Ranzone took Conry's phone. "Yes, Bill. How are you? What's up?"

"I know you're busy, John, but I wanted you to know I had a chat with a young man from the Innocence Project today who's working on the Swenson case."

Ranzone's heart sank. A few days had passed since they'd brushed off that guy from the Innocence Project; and the nagging concentration lapses and occasional chills had just about disappeared. He hadn't talked to Bill for months, except for a brief hello at the debate. But like Pavlov's bell, the words *Swenson case* shot a knot into his stomach. He didn't say a word.

Father Bill went on. "He seems to think Swenson's public defender was too inexperienced for a murder trial and that your state of mind at the time made it impossible for you to be fair."

"That's ridiculous. Where'd he get that idea?"

"He met Alice at the debate and somehow got that impression from her. She told him to talk to me."

"And what did you say?"

"Well, that's why I'm calling. I didn't think it was a big deal to tell him about mom's death. But I went into all that mess with Doug. I realize you try to keep him out of things so I thought you should know I may have made a mistake."

"No worries, Bill. That case was a no-brainer. Not even Johnny Cochrane could have won that one for Swenson. Sure, mom's death affected me, but not *that* much. And as far as Dougie goes, I'm not even sure where he lives now. I can't see anybody bringing him up. If I was running for President, maybe. But he won't be an issue. Don't worry; thanks for telling me."

The call ended and Ranzone stared out the window. His body tensed with the effort to keep shut the door to the dark basement where he had exiled the Swenson case. That case was like a psychic whack-a-mole. He just couldn't put it away for good. He had learned over the years to ignore the moans and occasional screams from the dark place and, by now, they were usually only exhausted whispers. But with so much on the line, even a whisper was nightmare material. And Father Bill's little talk with the Innocence Project was more than a whisper. Ranzone could almost hear banging on the door.

Ranzone asked the driver to find a rest room. Eight minutes later, they pulled off the Interstate to a Burger King where he rushed into the bathroom for a bout of dry heaves.

Chapter 13

Owen doubted that Ranzone's grief and hostile attitude was a legal reason to question the Swenson verdict, but it was certainly a *human* reason. As he drove away from the St Francis rectory he told himself that, if you combine Ranzone's state of mind with the apparent lie Phelan told about Swenson *not* owing him money, maybe this Swenson case deserves more work.

After a few miles of internal debate, he decided to call the Deputy Commissioner. Bill Kopinski had suggested he go to the Innocence Project in the first place, hadn't he? Shouldn't he be willing to help out a bit? It was after four which was usually the best time to reach Kopinski, so he called, reached him and, without too much persuasion, got him to agree to show Owen the police files on the case. Not the evidence in the evidence locker. Just the written files. And only in his office. Owen would be permitted to takes notes but would not be permitted to copy anything or take anything away.

Kopinski had suggested that Owen visit him at the lunch hour. He could have someone retrieve the file by then, and he'd order something from the deli to eat in his office while Owen worked. They wouldn't be bothered with staff wondering what Owen was doing.

The next day, Owen arrived a little before noon as Kopinski was finishing a meeting with a uniformed police officer. Some sort of disciplinary matter, apparently. He stood waiting outside Kopinski's open door, trying not to listen to his conversation and watching the large room in which he was waiting empty as everyone left for lunch.

Kopinski waved Owen into his office as he was escorting the uniform out; and pointed to a file on his desk. "You can use my desk. I'll sit over here and eat." No *how you been doin's* or *nice to see ya's.* But with Kopinski, Owen didn't expect those niceties. Kopinski grabbed a deli bag from his desk and went to sit in a wooden armchair in the corner. Owen sat at the desk, exhaled and began reading.

The basic story was not new to Owen by this point. On the morning of July 25th, 1992, the owner of that dry cleaners on Kensington Avenue had gone out his back door to dump some trash in his dumpster and noticed the dead woman in the alley running alongside the store. He called the police. They arrived with a team from forensics who estimated the victim's time of death at ten thirty p.m. or a little later the previous evening. Shortly after they arrived, they were approached by James Phelan who suggested they talk to Swenson who he'd seen near the dry cleaners late the previous evening. No mention of seeing the woman when he saw Swenson. No exact time.

Phelan directed the police to Swenson's room and when they awakened him and searched his premises, they found a knife and a wad of cash. Four hundred seventy-two dollars to be exact. Swenson seemed very nervous when he was interviewed, stuttering and sweating, and the police brought him to the local precinct station. When questioned about his whereabouts the previous evening, Swenson said he'd been to a Phillies game at the Vet and got home late. Asked if he knew a James Phelan, he said he did. When told Phelan reported seeing him near the murder site at about the time the woman was killed, Swenson acknowledged he had seen Phelan the previous evening, but had seen him almost two blocks from the dry cleaners and that it was closer to quarter to twelve when they passed each other on Kensington Avenue. Claimed Phelan was lying because Swenson hadn't paid him money he owed him. Swenson was held over pending further investigation.

The police spoke again to Phelan who insisted his previous statement had been accurate, adding that Swenson had been smoking and talking to an older woman when he saw him. And that Swenson did not owe him any money. There was no mention of that Greg Stuart who had claimed at the trial to have seen Swenson cleaning a knife at about the time of the murder. He apparently emerged at a later date. Nevertheless, the matter was turned over to the DA's office.

The report had been typed on a pre-printed form and all the space allocated for the basics was used up with the story leading to the referral to the DA's office. But there were two additional pages. One was an inventory of the items put into the evidence locker (cash, Phillies ticket stub for a July 24 night game with the Giants, and knife—recently cleaned but determined by lab to be the size used in the slaying). And the second page was a single paragraph typed on a plain white sheet with the heading "Link to Kensington Strangler?" That report began with a list of the ways in which the dry cleaning murder differed from the previous slayings by the so-call Kensington Strangler.

1. The Stanglers victims were all strangled with a nylon stocking. The bingo lady was stabbed to death.
2. The Strangler's victims were all raped. The dry cleaning lady was not.

3. While there were no eyewitness to the stranglings, all the unsubstantiated leads that surfaced suggested the Strangler was a medium sized, young man. Swenson was frail and thirty-eight.

The report then listed the ways in which the dry cleaning murder was similar to the Stranglings.

1. Killing occurred in the same general vicinity and the same time of night.

2. All victims were older women.

3. All Strangler victims had died with their hands folded around a piece of coal-like rock (identified by the lab as obsidianite). A similar rock was also found near the body of the dry cleaning lady. (Note to file: Neither the use of nylon stockings as a strangling weapon nor the coal findings were ever made public, to avoid false confessions and possible copy-cat killings).

Final Note: After reviewing the above, DA decided to prosecute only the dry cleaning murder. Concerned a conviction for the Stranglings would be more difficult than a conviction for the dry cleaning killing only. And if Swenson was the Strangler, fine.

Like all the other parts of the report, this last one was signed by *Lt. Det. Phillip Conry*.

Owen was surprised at the paucity of the evidence against Swenson. The most damning—at least before Greg Stuart's testimony later, at the trial—was Phelan's testimony. But Owen had already learned that testimony was at least partially untrue. Well, probably untrue. And didn't that Phillies ticket corroborate at least part of Swenson's story? What else could be used to demonstrate Swenson's innocence?

Owen put the skimpy file back in its folder and gave it a pat. "Not sure there's much here for me. But I appreciate the opportunity. Thanks."

Kopinski crumpled the wrappings from his lunch, and headed for the wastebasket alongside his desk. Owen popped up to let him take back his seat. As he was sitting down, Kopisnki asked "Anything in there suggesting Ranzone was a little off at the time?"

"No. Not really. But as I told you yesterday, the trial transcripts did. Maybe."

"Hmm. I didn't really know Ranzone back then. I was just starting with the detectives. He'd already gone to law school and was with the DA's office.

But I must say, he had a good reputation with the detectives, willing to dig in to his cases like he was still one of them. Most guys loved him for it."

"I'm sure they did."

"Yeah, but there were some rumors. I was in homicide and he'd been in vice, so I really can't say for sure. But some guys said that he made a sneaky deal to wangle law school."

"What do you mean? 'Wangle law school'?"

"Well, it's not unusual for cops to want to be lawyers. The only problem is time. They'd have to quit their jobs to go full time to law school; so most wanna-be lawyers ask to be transferred to a desk job so they can go to school at night. I assume you know that cops look down on desk jobs. You're not a real cop if you're working a desk."

"Okay. So what did Ranzone do?"

"Well, he managed to get his detective schedule adjusted each term to dovetail with his class schedule. Finished law school in only four years."

"So why is that a 'wangle'?"

"Well, the rumor is he caught his squad chief, I think his name was Calderone, in a drug scam. Confiscating drugs, putting some in the evidence locker but keeping half for himself and his guys to sell to known dealers in West Philly. When Ranzone heard about it, he negotiated his law school deal with Calderone and they all lived happily ever after."

"But isn't that a crime? I mean Ranzone keeping it secret?"

"Maybe, but not to the blue brotherhood. Ranzone was never part of the scheme. He was clean in that way. All he did was refuse to squeal. I'm sure a lot of cops would fault him for that; but a lot also see it as a kind of necessary loyalty." Kopinski slid the Swenson file back and forth on his desk with his eyes cast down before picking up his tale "As I say, it was always just a rumor. Who's to say he didn't convince Calderone of his case on its merits. I really don't know."

Owen had been standing through Kopinski's story and he wanted to sit down to catch his breath when it was finished. But instead, he simply reached across the desk for a handshake and thanked the Deputy Commissioner for his help.

Chapter 14

Owen waited a long time for the elevator on Kopinski's floor. Probably staff returning from lunch and getting off at every stop below. By the time he reached street level, his breath was labored. That news about Ranzone had upset him, disturbing the picture he had of a decent guy, family man and loving big brother who, at worst, had let his grief over his mother's death get the best of him for a while. More than twenty years ago, to boot. Paying little attention to his surroundings, he padded his way from Kopinski's Race Street office building to the Market East Station for his train back to Chestnut Hill. At Market East, he saw on the schedule board that his train was not for thirty-five minutes; so he grabbed some fruit and a smoothie and sat on a long bench to wait.

Slouching on the bench and sipping his smoothie in a kind of daze, he told himself that the rumor could be untrue, that Ranzone had indeed convinced Calderone to change his schedule without resort to some kind of blackmail. Or Calderone might have just liked him and wanted to help. Star athlete, personable, his father a cop. Calderone would've understood how Ranzone senior would have been mortified to have a son working at a precinct desk somewhere. All this could have been the case whether or not the rumors about Calderone were true in the first place. As Kopinski'd said, his negotiation might have succeeded on its own merits. Maybe the schedule adjustments were not that significant. Finally, Owen realized that, whatever the truth of the Calderone affair, it all happened years before the Swenson case and could not possibly have a bearing on it.

But still.

On the train back to Chestnut Hill, Owen forced himself to ignore the later testimony of Greg Stuart about the knife cleaning and focus on the Swenson file he'd read at Kopinski's. Most of it rehashed what he already knew; although there were two vague possibilities that should make him feel a little better about working for Swenson. First was that Phelan's testimony got more damning over time. Either he was just remembering more facts each time the police interviewed him; or he found out about Swenson's cash and gotten madder and madder as he thought about Swenson's lie to him. Either way, it was too late to cross-examine him now.

The second finding was that Swenson had apparently actually gone to a Phillies game that night. And the police had apparently never shown that ticket stub to Peter Martin. That in itself could be a help to Swenson. And depending on when the game ended and whether he'd stayed to the end, he may or may not have had time to be where Phelan says he spotted him. Baseball records being as comprehensive as they are, it should not be too hard to check the details of that game and test Swenson's memory of them.

It was about two-thirty when Owen finished his walk home from the Chestnut Hill station and he concluded he had enough time to research that Phillies game before the kids arrived; so he gave Barb a perfunctory kiss hello and rushed to his office to sit at his computer.

The Internet always amazed Owen. Whatever you wanted to know, it was there, like talking to God. And as he'd hoped, he had no trouble finding the details of that July 24th game. The Phillies played the Giants and won 8 to 4. At the time, the Phillies were in last place in their division, eleven games out, so the crowd was a sparse 20,580. It was a very long game, three hours and forty-five minutes, which would mean that, given the usual 7:05 start time, the game couldn't have ended until ten fifty. With so few people in attendance, it wouldn't have taken Swenson more than ten or fifteen minutes to walk from the Vet to the subway at Broad and Pattison. If he had taken the express from there, he couldn't have gotten to the connection for the El until, maybe, eleven fifteen, eleven twenty. And if he took the local from Broad and Pattison, it would have been even later. The ride on the El to the Tioga street stop in Kensington could have taken, what, twenty minutes at the least? That would put Swenson on Kensington Avenue at about twelve to twelve thirty, just as he'd claimed.

Owen felt a twitter of hope until he realized that Swenson might not have stayed to the very end of the game. Whenever Owen went to a sporting event, he would be chagrined by the number of people who left early. While most of them just seemed intent on beating the traffic away from the stadium, the car-less Swenson could have been one of those fans who leave when they think the game is effectively over. All he could do was test Swenson's memory of the game. See how long he might have stayed. He called the prison and arranged a phone conference with Swenson for the following morning.

The first thing Owen wanted to talk about was the testimony of that Greg Stuart. About cleaning the knife.

"Charles, tell me about that guy who saw you cleaning you knife?"

"G . . . g . . . reg? Yeah, he seen m . . . m . . . me. But I c . . . c . . . clean my knife every n. .n. night." In painfully halting fashion, Swenson explained that he used the knife for everything, including cutting up fruit. So he kept it clean. And washed it with soap and water every night. "An' re . . . m . . . member. They didn't find no b . . . b . . . blood anywheres."

Owen felt his stomach drop. Why hadn't Swensen been this definitive when Peter Martin asked him about Stuart? Had he decided in the intervening years to tighten up his story? Rather than cross-examine, he moved on to the Phillies game.

Swenson's Phillies story was sound. He stayed till the end of the game because he went to so few of them and wanted to enjoy every minute. That and he'd hoped to see Mitch Williams pitch at the end. "You re . . . m . . . member M . . . m . . . mitch Williams, don't you? Or are you t . . . t . . . too young? He was the Phillies c . . . c . . . closer at the time and I loved him. That cr . . . cr . . . crazy hair. I was happy when F . . . F . . . Fregosi put him in to shut the Giants d . . . down."

So far, so good, Owen thought. From what he'd learned from the Internet, Mitch Williams had in fact gotten the save as the closer for the game. But had Swenson studied up on the game to fortify his phony alibi?

"You sure you stayed to the final out?"

"Ab . . . b . . . bsolutely. I remember bein' n . . . n . . . nervous that if the game didn't end s. . s. soon, I'd miss the El. They were sh. . sh. .uttin' it down 'bout midnight. I d . . . d . . . didn't want to take the b . . . b . . . bus they put in its place. It would t . . . t . . . take too long to get home. But it all wo . . . wo . . . worked out. I ma . . . ma . . . made the El in time."

Owen had checked the subway and El schedules and found, in fact, that midnight to five-thirty service on the El was discontinued the year before the night in question.

"Did the police ask you anything about the game? Did you tell them you stayed to the end?"

"They d . . . d . . . didn't ask. Wa . . . wa . . . why? Is it important?"

That last question got to Owen. Either Swenson's ingenuousness was a sign of innocence or he was more skillful at deception than Owen would have thought. Opting for the first interpretation, he decided to question Conry. If he could reach him.

Chapter 15

It took Owen four frustrating calls to Conry's voicemail before Conry finally answered. He must have recognized Owen's number.

"Mr. Delaney. What do you want now?"

"Just a couple more questions about the Swenson case."

"How'd I guess? I've only got a few minutes, so make it quick, please."

Owen asked him if he realized that Swenson's being where Phelan said he saw him at the time he said he saw him was impossible, given the lateness of the Phillies game. Conry said they knew the game went late, but just assumed Swenson left early.

"Did you question him about the game? Details about the ending?"

"Not that I recall. But by morning a Phillies fan would have known those details whether he went to the game or not. What else you want to know?"

Owen reported his conversation with Marge Swenson and asked whether or not Conry thought Swenson owing Phelan money could have colored his story about that night.

"Not really. First off, it's been more than twenty years. Phelan's wife couldn't possibly remember such a detail now. And even if it was true, Phelan could have been trying to distance himself from Swenson. Afraid we might think he was a good buddy, even an accomplice. I don't think whether or not Swenson owed him money makes any difference at all."

"Okay, but I wonder if you guys would have charged Swenson if you hadn't found that obsidiante that tied him to the Kensington Stranglings."

Conry said nothing for ten seconds before asking "How'd you know about that?"

"I read your incident file."

Conry blew into his phone. "I won't ask how you managed that. But what you don't know is that Swenson was arrested way before we found that piece of obsidi ... whatever. That piece of coal. So the answer to your question is obviously yes, we not only would have but we *did* arrest him without that piece of evidence."

"Can you explain a little more? When did you find the piece of coal?"

"Actually, I didn't find it. The prosecuting DA did."

"John Ranzone?"

"Right. He was a great one for checking the scenes of the crimes he was assigned to prosecute. By the time he got the assignment, Swenson was in custody. I think we arrested him on a Saturday morning. And John went up to Kensington with me on Monday. Swenson was arraigned a couple days later."

"But the piece of coal was never entered into evidence."

"Right. John was sure he could get a conviction without it. Besides, we had no other good evidence to tie him to the stranglings and John was worried the coal could be a distraction; particularly since we found it a couple days after the murder and it wasn't in the victim's hand like it was in the stranglings. But when we found it, we knew we'd got the Strangler."

Conry didn't point out that the stranglings stopped once Swenson was taken in but Owen couldn't hold back a final dejected "And the Stranglings stopped once you had him."

"Exactly." Conry paused and said "Listen, I got to go. Hope this conversation is our last."

Owen had been at home when he talked to Conry. Barb was out and he wanted to talk to someone about his Swenson dilemma, so he called Bob Glassman at the Innocence Project. Glassman took his call and asked how the case was going.

"That's what I wanted to talk about. I'm not sure this case is worth our time."

"Okaaay." Glassman sounded a little bored. "Tell me about it."

Owen had prepared what he thought of as a short brief before calling Glassman. He would start with Ranzone's state of mind at the time of the trial and the inexperience of Swenson's public defender. Then he would go into the way the angry and aggressive Ranzone overwhelmed Peter Martin with evidence that Owen now considered dubious, though not convincingly so. Finally, he'd seek some guidance on the big question of whether or not the Innocence Project should put in effort to free a man imprisoned for a murder he might not have committed when the same man had murdered others without ever being punished. He felt comfortable with his opening bit on Ranzone's state of mind.

"The first thing to know is that Ranzone's mother died a few days before the Kensington slaying. Her funeral was on the 22nd of July, the slaying on the evening of July 24. When Ranzone's youngest brother—his name's Doug—didn't show up for the funeral, Ranzone and his other brother, Bill, went to Doug's house in Olney to confront him. They hadn't been to the house in years. What they found were signs that Doug had become a heavy drinker and a kind of degenerate. John was upset, with Doug, but apparently more so with himself for letting Doug slide into that state. John had been Doug's protector for most of Doug's life but had become less attentive in the years before their mother's death."

"Hold on one second, Owen. How did you learn all this?"

"I talked to his brother, Bill, who is a priest, by the way."

"Okay. Continue."

"I say Ranzone was upset; but it was more like he was furious with what seemed to be a combination of grief and anger. At one point he took a baseball bat and swept it across the top of Doug's dresser, smashing a big jar of gemstones called Apache Tears in the process."

Glassman interrupted with a laugh. "Haven't heard that term in years. My son had a collection of Apache Tears when he was younger. Dug them up on a vacation out west, Arizona, I think. You know the legend about them?"

"Yeah, the widowed Apache squaws crying over their slain husbands. Tears falling to the ground and forming the gemstones. Father Bill told me about it."

"Right, that's the story. But Apache Tears are by no means gemstones. Some people shine them up to look good; but they're really just pieces of obsidianite and look like a piece of coal if you don't work on them. My son never did anything with them and my wife finally threw them out."

Owen felt his stomach drop. His mind raced in the seconds of silence that followed. *How many households in Philadelphia had a collection of Apache Tears?*

Probably a good number.

How many of those households were in the Olney, Frankford, Kensington area where family vacations out west were less common? At least in the late 1980s?

A lot fewer.

How many of those collections were kept by adult males?

Probably very few.

And how many of those males were intellectually limited, heavy drinkers, loners obsessed with sex who had difficult relationships with their sixty-some year-old mothers?

Maybe just one.

"You still there, Owen?"

"Yes. I was going to tell you about some flaws I've found in the DA's evidence. But. . . . you should know that I saw in the police report that they found a lump of obsidianite at the crime scene and that a piece of obsidianite was also squeezed into the hands of the Strangler's victims. Not only that, but that obsidiante was found by John Ranzone, not the police. A few days after Swenson's arrest."

"So, what are you saying, Owen? That John Ranzone planted some obsidianite at the scene to get a conviction and then never used it in the trial? That doesn't make sense."

"No. What I'm saying is that John Ranzone planted an *Apache Tear* at the crime scene to protect his brother."

PART II
ON HIS OWN

Chapter 16

"Okay. To start with, I think we have to assume that John Ranzone knew the unpublished details of the Kensington Stranglings, the stockings and the obsidianite."

Owen was leaning forward from the edge of the leather chair in Glassman's office. Glassman had summoned him after he'd dropped the Ranzone bombshell the previous afternoon.

Glassman said "Okay. Go on."

"And I believe that when he saw how his brother was living after not having been to that house for a number of years, saw the drawer full of stockings and the Apache Tears, knowing that Doug was a little off and always had been, and that he had a troubled relationship with his mother, he became immediately suspicious that Doug was the Strangler. No wonder he was enraged."

"Of course he could have been enraged for the reasons Father Bill suspected, not because he thought Doug was the Strangler."

"Well, sure. But that funeral was on July 22. The dry cleaning stabbing was discovered on the 25th in the same general vicinity as the stranglings. When John heard about it, I bet he asked to be assigned to the case so he'd have an excuse to visit the crime scene with Detective Conry. He got the case and went to inspect the scene on the 27th. That's when he miraculously found the obsidianite, the Apache Tear, which had not been noticed by forensics on the 25th. That oversight by forensics seems unlikely to me. I think Ranzone planted it. I'm surprised he didn't also find a woman's stocking somewhere down that alley." Owen was tempted to stand and pace about the room; but he just inched further forward in his chair. "And then, to cap it all off, he gets Doug out of town. So the Kennsington Stranglings stopped and Swenson ended up looking like the Strangler."

Glassman rocked in his huge desk chair. His face looked like he smelled something unpleasant. "All right, Owen. That's essentially what you hypothesized yesterday." Glassman stopped rocking and leaned forward, elbows on his desk. "But I should tell you, Owen, that I called Deputy Commissioner Kopinski yesterday after we spoke. Told him what you thought."

"And?"

"He said that you were given to flights of fancy sometimes. And he was afraid that his telling you the rumor about Ranzone and that guy Calderone may have poisoned your thinking, that it may have set you off on one of your flights."

Owen leaned back and sighed. Sure, he had a wild imagination. And sometimes his imaginings were pure fantasy. But not this time. He was positive.

"Did Kopinski also tell you that my so-called flights of fantasy often proved to be accurate descriptions of what actually happened? That they helped solve actual crimes?"

"Yes. He did throw in some compliments. But I've spent some time thinking through your theory and I have a lot of questions."

"Such as?"

"Well, if Ranzone thought his brother was the Strangler, why not just send him out of town? Remove the possibility that he'd be caught?"

"That's easy. He needed the Kennsington Strangler case to be effectively closed. Without creating the impression that Swenson was the Strangler, ongoing investigations into the stranglings might have lead to Doug, no matter where he was."

"Okay, then why not accuse Swenson of the stranglings, convict him and close the case for real? He could still move his brother if he thought Doug might commit more stranglings."

"Well, my view is that John was correct when he questioned the possibility of convicting Swenson of the stranglings. He knew that case was weak. I doubt he, himself, suspected Swenson was the Strangler. But he also knew that if he got a conviction in the Swenson case and the stranglings stopped, the whole world soon draw the conclusion that Swenson was the Strangler, particularly since the insiders knew about the obsidianite and wouldn't challenge that impression. And if he moved Dougie and the stranglings didn't stop, he could move Dougie back to Philadelphia and live happily ever after. So what he did was fudge the evidence in the Swenson case—or at least fail to do a complete job or turn over every thing he had to the public defender—bully his way to a conviction and move Doug out of town. The Stranglings did stop. And now everyone assumes Ranzone had put away the Strangler. Two birds with one stone."

Glassman leaned back, crossed his legs and interlaced his hands around his knee. He bowed his head slightly, staring at his hands. He said nothing for fifteen or twenty seconds and Owen took that to mean Glassman was coming around. But when he uncoiled and sat back, he said "And how does all this help Swenson? That's our job isn't it? I don't think what you seem to think of as new evidence is very convincing. A woman's vague assumption that Swenson probably did owe money to her husband on a specific date over twenty years ago? Not very powerful. And the Phillies game? That might be a little stronger. Ranzone *should* have shared the existence of that ticket stub with the public defender. But I doubt it would have made much difference if he had. It's more than two decades after the game and you were able to learn all the details about it on the Internet without any problem. How much easier would it to have been for Swenson to check the details the morning after the game. He could have left early, been at the crime scene when his friend claimed he was, and had those details ready if he was asked. Had this attorney raised the game as a defense during the trial, I think Ranzone could have convincingly made that argument. And you haven't got any explanation about Swenon's cleaning his knife except that he says he did it every night."

Glassman thumped his elbows on his desk and crossed his arms. He shook his head almost unnoticeably, a grey haired pendulum swinging to a dirge-like rhythm. "Here's where I come down, Owen. We're the Innocence Project, not the Guilty Project. I don't think you've brought us anything that proves Swenson's innocence. We have to drop the case. And as far as Ranzone goes, we're not prosecutors and have no way to pursue your theory about him, even if it were true. If we tried, our funders would probably disown us. Stick to your lane, they'd say." He twisted his mouth slightly when he finished, as though he hadn't wanted to say what he had just said.

"Owen, if you really believe your Ranzone theory, you'd have to go to the DA. Ta dah! Lots of luck with that."

Chapter 17

John Ranzone was napping when Phil Conry tapped on his hotel room door. He rolled to the side of his bed and shakily stood up to grab a robe from the nearby armchair. He felt woozy. Head rush. Probably blood pressure. He padded to the door, heard Conry say "It's Phil, John," opened it and led Conry to a cheap, walnut veneered table set against the wall. Conry pulled up a second chair and they sat next to each other. No seating areas in these basic Holiday Inn rooms; but that was the best they could get in Oil City.

Conry never seemed to tire. He wanted to go over their agenda for the next few days. Ranzone would have been happy to limit the discussion to one day; but Conry rambled on as John tried to clear his head. When Conry finished with the details of the rally in Pittsburg in three days, he closed his file.

"Looks like you could use some more sleep, John. Sorry to've bothered you; but there's a ton of speeches in the next few days. I think we've chosen the right themes for the audiences you'll face. So please, don't change any of them without a little chat." Conry stood to leave; but said "Oh, and John, I think we're done with that guy from the Innocence Project. Spoke to him today, told him about that obsidianite, or whatever it was, and he seemed satisfied."

Ranzone felt woozy again. "What about it?"

"He thought we might have been less aggressive, maybe not even arrested Swenson, if we hadn't found that lump of coal and thought he was the Strangler. So I told him what happened, that we felt our case was good enough to arrest him before finding the coal; that we didn't find it until a couple days after the arrest; that you were a very thorough assistant DA and you found it when you checked out the crime scene with me a couple days after the arrest." Conry tilted his slightly bowed his head and extended his open palms to his side, like he was expecting applause. Then he said "I told him we all considered the piece of coal proof Swenson was the Strangler; but you didn't want to risk a conviction by charging him with everything he'd done. And you were right." He backed to the door and winked, "have a good nap, John."

When Conry closed the door behind him, Ranzone staggered to his bed and threw himself down, face first. He wanted to cry—or scream, he didn't know which. For years, when the case would surface to a conscious level and he could hear the moans behind that basement door, he'd told himself what he'd done wasn't that bad. Unless Swenson was innocent, of course, which he doubted. And there really was no proof that Dougie had anything to do with the stranglings. But he felt like punching Conry for telling the Innocence Project that he was the one who'd found that Apache Tear. He wanted to be no part of that story. He'd reviewed Conry's report at every stage back then to make sure he was left out of it. But damn, stupid Phil had sure fucked that up.

He rolled on to his back and stared at the ceiling, taking several deep breaths to relieve the tightness in his chest. When he calmed himself down, he told himself that maybe Conry was right, that the Innocence Project was satisfied.

Chapter 18

Outside Glassman's office, Owen fished his phone from his pants pocket to call Barbara. But he didn't call. He knew she would be sympathetic to his loss of the Swenson case; but her apprehension about his exposing himself to danger would probably prevent her from recognizing the moral dilemma in which he found himself. No point in upsetting her with it; but he couldn't put it out of his mind. He tried his old standby in tough choice situations, the big mistake/small mistake analysis. But the problem was that too many choices could end in big mistakes. If he went public with his suspicions about Ranzone and they were wrong, he'd not only probably affect the campaign and deny the state the services of a good man, but would also make himself out to be a kook. Not to mention what it would do to Dougie. If Ranzone had done what he suspected him of doing and he said nothing, an unworthy criminal would probably be elected governor of his state and a possibly innocent Swenson would spend the rest of his life in prison.

Owen wandered toward the Delaware River waterfront, which like so much of Philadelphia, was revitalized with new commerce and new residences. Actually, he thought he liked it better as it was when he was growing up. More evidence of authentic river life.

He took one of the pedestrian overpasses across I 95 to Penn's Landing and found a bench with a good water view. The bench was empty and few people were nearby. But had a complete stranger sat down next to him, he would have been tempted to discuss the Ranzone problem, so great was his need to talk. What he really needed was some moral guidance. Father Bill might understand; but of course, he was out of the question. He could not think of a single cleric whom he had befriended in his life. So he started on a list of friends who had been of help in his previous cases. He guessed it was reasonable at this point to call them "cases".

Other than Barb whom he didn't want to alarm, she seemed so happy that he was pursuing his hobby without risking life or limb, there was Sam Kaufman. He'd known Sam since grade school at Germantown Friends where Sam had been a boy computer genius. He'd ended up a full-grown computer genius and taught at Owen's university. Problem was that, though he was a master of the digital world, he was sometimes a dunce in the human one. Owen could not see getting help with a moral dilemma from Sam.

Then there was Rick Jennings, also an old schoolmate. Rick had been both a great athlete and a sensitive reader of poetry and what you might call classic introspective novels, like George Elliot's or Anthony Trollope's. The old Rick would have been perfect; but he'd somehow slid into the frantic life of a big-time New York City lawyer before being hired as the well-paid in-house counsel for a multinational based in Pittsburg. Owen guessed that his career had exposed him to too many compromises for him to recognize a moral dilemma when he saw one. For all Owen knew, Rick had been a big contributor to the Ranzone Campaign.

Then he thought of Geoff Shultz, a math teacher at Community College with whom he occasionally tutored promising students who had a good shot at getting into a major university like the one at which Owen taught. He'd missed several semesters of tutoring and hadn't chatted with Geoff for a while. Even though Geoff was a world class cynic, Owen had been impressed with his sensitivity when dealing with the students they both tutored, Geoff in Math and Owen in basic English. And Geoff had been wonderful helping Owen interview an older woman teacher at Community who had critical information in one of Owen's early cases.

Owen stood and walked back over I 95 to Front Street where he thumbed his Uber app and set his destination for Community College.

Owen had no idea whether or not Geoff would be free; and when he found himself outside Geoff's classroom/office, he could see through the door that a class was in session. And he could understand just about every full-throated word the basso voiced Shultz was saying. At one point while Geoff was demonstrating a proof on his whiteboard, he noticed Owen, smiled and held up five fingers. The class was soon dismissed and Owen stood back from the door as students grabbed their backpacks and filed out. He entered when the little parade was over. Shultz was the first to speak. His voice was as big as ever, as though he were talking to someone way down the hall.

"Hey stranger. Where ya been? You're not tutoring this semester are you?"

"No. No tutoring this semester. In fact, I'm on sabbatical. I just wanted to talk. Got a few minutes?"

"Well, as a matter of fact, I have an hour break which, as I recall, is about what you need for a few minute conversation."

"Funny. But you're right. This probably will take some time."

Owen sat in a student desk looking up at Geoff who had taken a seat on the stool behind his teaching podium. Owen sighed, shook his head and told his story. It took about forty-five minutes to get from his first chat with Kopinski to his being dismissed by Glassman earlier that day.

Shultz slid off his stool and, saying nothing, sat down in the student desk next to Owen. Owen half-expected Shultz to tell him to forget the whole thing, that the problem was too big, too complex, too important, for him to mess around with. But Shultz surprised him.

"What the fuck are you gonna do?" Shultz's tone was conversational which, for him, was, a virtual whisper; and it resonated with genuine empathy, like he was consoling a child whose dog had died.

"I have no clue. That's why I came here to talk."

Shultz curled himself into the desk, crossing his arms and legs and bowing his head. After a few seconds he said "I think you should try to find Ranzone's kid brother. Doug, was it?"

"Why? What would that do for me?" Owen stood.

"Well, assuming he's still alive, you might be able to sound him out about those stranglings. From what you say, he's a marginal sort of guy. If he is the Strangler, he's probably been scared shitless for twenty plus years that someone would find out. That should come through if you talk to him." Shultz shifted in his seat to face Owen who had stood and begun to pace. "One way or another, it might help you decide what to do. If he feels guilty to you, maybe you should push your Ranzone theory on some authorities up here. At least you'd have all the pieces of the puzzle for them."

Owen had stopped in a corner and was leaning against the wall. Shultz shifted again to address him. "And if you don't get those guilty vibes, maybe your theory is all wrong."

Owen returned to the student desk next to Shultz and sat down. "Maybe you're right. But I'm not sure I'd be as perceptive as you think I'd be. This isn't like asking my kids if they snuck some of the candies Barb hid in the cupboard. I'm sure I could read their reactions to that. But this Douglas is a grown man and the whole thing seems too important for me to be going on hunches."

"Well, if it turns out to be just a hunch, you're probably dead in the water. But remember, this grown man may still be a kid emotionally. Or intellectually, from what that priest told you. Never know what he'll say. And besides, what other choices have you got? You could do nothing, which would kill you, with your compulsion to right every wrong. Or you could confront John Ranzone himself, which would be pointless. Or you talk to the brother. It's only he and John who know the truth, and maybe not even John"

Owen rested his left elbow on the desktop and cupped his chin in that hand while drumming on the desktop with the other. He mumbled into his hand, half to himself and half to Shultz, "Maybe. But to do it properly, I'd have to be face to face with him."

"Right. That would increase the odds that you'd end up with something more than a hunch. But in person or on the phone, you still have to find him first."

Owen slumped in his seat and stared ahead. He noticed a laptop on Shultz's desk. "May I use your computer?"

"Sure."

Owen stood and strode to Geoff's desk and opened the computer. Then he logged into his *PeopleSearch* account and asked it to find all the Douglas Ranzones in the country. To his surprise, there was only one. While the age of that Ranzone, late fifties, was about right, the *PeopleSearch* Doug lived out west and had a large family. No chance he was the one. The droop of Owen's shoulders told Shultz all he had to know. He had been sitting at attention while Owen did his research; but understanding what happened, he folded himself back into his thinking crouch and went quiet for a while until he took a deep breath and unfolded again.

"Do you think Father Bill would know the names of Ranzone's friends who were supposed to look out for Doug down in Florida? That might be a start."

"Good idea. Maybe. I should ask. I'll call him."

Owen began scrolling through the recent calls on his phone but stopped when the classroom door opened and two students entered, apparently for Geoff's next class. He put his phone back in his pocket and said "I'll do this at home Geoff. But thanks; you've been a help."

On his train ride home, Owen had second thoughts about calling Father Bill. How would he possibly explain to the priest his reason for wanting those names, even assuming Father Bill knew them?

As the train passed through the Queen Lane station, there was a gaggle of Germantown Friends School students waiting for their train home to Center City. Young enough to still hold idealistic Quaker notions about honesty, they made him feel even more queasy about a bald-faced lie to Father Bill. The good father had been so forthcoming the last time they talked that Owen hated to be less than open with him. But, if he *did* lie, found Doug, and then found that his theory was wrong, no harm would be done. Finding Doug might even result in some good since no one in the family seemed to know where he was. And if somehow he found his theory was correct, it would be worth the little lie, despite the pain it would cause the Ranzone family.

Owen decided that a partial truth was the best way to lie to Father Bill. When he got home, he'd call Father Bill, tell him the half truth that he was still working on the Swenson case and wanted to reach Doug to get Doug's take on John's state of mind at the time of the Swenson trial.

The half-lie worked.

Father Bill remembered those friends because they had been on John's college baseball team. And, since John had not minded his talking to Owen the last time, he doubted he'd have any problem with Owen's request. "But remember, Owen, even if you find Doug—and none of us have been able to reach him for years—he probably won't be much help. He was in bad psychological shape himself at the time. He was essentially going through a withdrawal while he stayed with me at the rectory in North Wales. Never even left the building. And even as a kid, he wasn't what you'd call psychologically observant, particularly about John who could do no wrong in his eyes."

So Father Bill gave Owen two names, Carl Watson and John Zapotosky; but he cautioned Owen not to get his hopes up.

Owen did not know what he would do without PeopleSearch.com. It had become almost a universal rolodex for him. Want to find an address and landline phone number? For anyone, anywhere? Look it up on *PeopleSearch*. The only drawback with the system, a problem getting increasingly worse each year, was that the system did not show cell phone numbers.

He decided to try Zapotosky first. Florida only. Should be fewer of them than Watsons. There were two J. Zapotoskys, one in Key West and one in Bradenton, both about Ranzone's age. The Key West number was no longer in operation—another likely conversion to exclusive cell phone use—but the Bradenton number was connected to a voice mail system. He left a message asking Mr. Zapotosky to call, saying he was a private detective from Philadelphia. He hoped that would be tantalizing enough to get a call back if he was the right Zapatosky; but he was afraid to mention John Ranzone, fearful that Zapotosky might try to reach Ranzone before returning the call. Owen didn't want that.

Owen went 0 for 4 with the age appropriate Carl Watsons scattered around the state. None of the published numbers were still working. If the Watsons had lived anywhere near Philadelphia, he could have driven to the listed addresses and knocked on doors like he'd done with Mrs. Phelan. But Florida was twelve hundred miles away. All he could do was wait and hope for a callback from the Bradenton Zapotosky. And hope that he was Ranzone's old teammate. And hope that the partial truth he planned to tell him, if he was the right Zapotosky, would not be too obvious a lie.

The callback came in the late afternoon. Owen took the call in his office with a clean yellow writing pad in front of him. Again, a partial truth/lie worked. Owen told Zapotosky that he was a detective trying to find Doug Ranzone, that Father Bill had told him Zapotosky might have some helpful information. That seemed to be enough for Zapotosky.

"I'm not sure I can be of any help. I can't even remember the last time I saw Doug. When he first came down here, Carl Watson and I helped him find a job with the road department. Carl was a friend from Pennsylvania, too.

"Anyway, things went okay for a while. Dougie had some money from the sale of his Philly house and bought an old pick-up and a beat-up house trailer with just enough room for one person. He rented a spot at a trailer park on 41, up a ways toward Sarasota, and lived there for at least five years. He'd call every once in a while; but I was never able to get a number for him. He always used a pay phone. I don't think he ever had a phone, though maybe now he's got a cheap cell. So it was hard to keep tabs on him without driving to that trailer park. I did that a few times; but he didn't show much enthusiasm when I showed up, so I stopped going after a while. About five years, as I said. Don't know if he's still there or not. Don't even know if he's still alive. He was always a little fragile. And he did have a drinking problem."

"Do you remember the name of the trailer park, Mr. Zapotosky?"

"Please, call me Zapo. People've calling me that since grade school. But to answer your question, I don't recall the name. Think it was Belmont or Bel Meade, something like that. On the east side of 41, south of Bradenton a ways."

"And the last time you saw or spoke to him was when?"

"Maybe 1997-98. I tried to keep up. For his brother's sake. John was a great friend. But Dougie made it almost impossible. Make sure you tell the family I did my best."

"What about Carl Watson? Think he could help?"

"Maybe he could've. But he died about three years ago."

"Does he have a family? They might know something."

"He has a son. Still lives in Punta Gorda, I think. Let me see if I have his number." Owen could hear Zapo's phone clunk on a hard surface. He waited almost three minutes before Zapo returned, panting noticeably.

"Couldn't find it. Sorry. Actually I did find three numbers, all scratched out. His mom was murdered maybe fifteen, twenty years ago, strangled one night out shopping, and it sent both him and his dad into a tailspin. Carl Senior was never the same and Carl Junior began bouncing from job to job. Never quite settled down again. Don't think he ever married."

"Thanks, Zapo. You've been a big help." Owen hoped that what he'd just said to Zapo was actually true.

Owen googled trailer parks near Bradenton, Florida, and found only one with a Bel in its name. Bel Aire, on route 41. He called and asked if a Doug Ranzone lived there. The deep, wheezy voice that answered told Owen that they didn't give out the names of their residents. "Sorry" he said, and hung up.

Owen bit a cheek and tapped his pencil on the still almost empty yellow pad. South of Bradenton, on the way to Sarasota. He then called up a map of southwest Florida and saw that the distance between Bradenton and Sarasota was not more than ten miles. He had been to Sarasota with his family some Christmases ago. Visiting Mama Colgrove, his stepmother, or whatever you called the second wife of your natural father who never acknowledged you as his child. Whatever.

But he'd also gone to Sarasota that Christmas to meet I.D. Pinkett, father of a graduate student killed at his university whose murder he'd helped solve. I.D. was a retired Sarasota police chief, one of and perhaps *the* first person of color to hold that position. Would he be able to help get past the gate at the Bel Aire trailer park? Owen still had I.D.'s number and he called.

Owen gave I.D. a rough outline of the story. While he said nothing to accuse Ranzone of wrongdoing, he did mention that he was looking for the brother of John Ranzone and had hit a dead end at the Bel Aire Trailer Park.

I.D. had no clue who Ranzone was. When Owen explained, I.D whistled into the phone, "Sounds like you hit the big time, boy."

Owen could picture I.D. Brown, almost reddish skin. Avuncular. Throwing back his shoulders, eyes wide.

"Yeah. But I feel like I'm over my head. And I could use your help."

"How so, Delaney? Want me to poke around that Bel Aire place? Maybe flash an old chief's card? Hope they don't check the dates?"

"Well, that's sort've what I had in mind." Owen was hoping that I.D still felt indebted to him for his work on his daughter's case.

I.D. was quiet for a while, then said "Sure. Why not? Got our golf game tomorrow but I'll go there soon as I can." Owen gave I.D. the information he thought he'd need and thanked him repeatedly before ending the call.

Chapter 19

Zapo's called the Ranzone land-line just as John and Elizabeth were finishing dinner at home in Philadelphia's East Falls neighborhood. The neighborhood had for years been home to the city's political movers and shakers, a quick drive into Center City along the West River Drive and a nice enough area, but not as posh as Chestnut Hill, say, which might have been off-putting to voters. The meal was one of the few John and Elizabeth had eaten together anywhere during the campaign. They couldn't even remember the last time they had sat at the dining room table. Elizabeth answered the call in the kitchen where she was getting desert. From the dining room, Ranzone could hear her end of the conversation.

"Zapo! So great to hear from you. It's been a long time." It took Elizabeth several minutes of effusive catching up before she called to John that Zapo was on the phone for him. John said he'd take the call in the den.

"Zapo, old friend! To what do I owe this great pleasure?"

"Oh John, I thought a lot about you today after I spoke to your private detective and figured I should call to wish you luck with the campaign. We don't get much Pennsylvania news down here; but my brother in York says things are looking good for you."

Ranzone's felt woozy at the mention of a private detective, disoriented, like he was about to faint. He shook his head to clear the fuzziness. What the hell was that about? Why did Zapo say *your* private detective? He didn't want to suggest he was in the dark about it; so he didn't respond. Save those questions for a little later.

"Yeah Zapo. Polls all look good and, believe it or not, I enjoy the campaign. It can be tiring and I feel run down a lot. But all in all, it's been great fun. Like winning a game that's been pretty well decided by the seventh inning."

The mention of baseball sent Zapo off on a string of reminiscences about their college days which, with each minute, got Ranzone's right leg bouncing more frantically. After what felt like an endless ramble by Zapo, Ranzone finally squeezed in an agreement about about those great old days and managed a shift in the conversation.

"So Zapo, tell me how it went with that detective."

"Not much to tell, John. I told him I hadn't seen Dougie since maybe 1997 or '98 when he lived in that trailer park on 41. You remember."

At the mention of his brother's name, Ranzone stiffened. So that was it. The Swenson case again. But how did the Innocence Project reach down to Florida? Holding a deep breath before speaking, he said "Yeah, I remember. What was it called again?"

"I didn't remember the name but I told him I thought it was Bel something. Belmont or BelMeade."

"Yeah, that sounds familiar; but he moved from there didn't he? I feel so bad that I've lost track. But he never kept us informed."

"I feel the same way, John. I'm glad you're trying to find him. Frankly, I'm guessing he could use some help, if he' still even alive." Zapo paused. John thought he might be worrying that his comment was inappropriate, so he said "Who knows, Zapo? Sad story."

"That it is, John." Another pause. "By the way John did you know that Carl died?"

"No! I didn't know that. What happened?"

"Well I guess technically it was a stroke. But he had given up on himself since his wife was murdered. Just couldn't get himself together. Ate too much, drank too much, you name it."

"His wife was murdered?"

"Yeah. She was strangled by a mugger after doing her shopping at a Publix down on 41 late one night. Must have been ten or more years ago. They never caught the guy."

"Oh boy," said John. "Hate to end the call on that note, but I really have to get to some campaign work."

When the call ended, John leaned forward in his armchair and held his head in his hands, telling himself that Doug couldn't possibly have anything to do with the strangling of Carl's wife. He shouldn't jump to conclusions. But damn that Conry. So stupid to have told the Innocence Project about him and that Apache Tear. They were obviously hunting for Dougie. Phil should have known to keep him out of the story. Now he had to do something about it. But what.

His first thought, to fire Phil, the only link between him and the Apache Tear and the Innocence Project guy. But that made no sense. Phil was a decent guy, a friend since they were both detectives on the vice squad, Phil a newbe and he more seasoned. Phil had looked up to him, maybe even hero-worshiped him was the better description. Phil had defended him against the Calderone rumors and had given up his detective job to sign on to the campaign for long-term prospects in state government. But Phil was still a boy scout; and that had to eventually get him into trouble in the world of politics. He probably should never have recruited him for the campaign. But what would firing Phil get him. Phil would still know what he knew. And how would he explain a firing? To Phil or to the world?

No, he had to make sure Phil never spoke of the Swenson case again. But how should he do that? Phil was an impossible target for a threat. What could he be threatened with? He was too clean for any sort of smear, which would hurt the campaign in any event. And, if the Apache Tear ever came up in a Swenson re-trial, Phil would never lie under oath. Even if John pleaded. But if Phil could be neutralized, there would be nothing and no one to say he'd planted that Apache Tear. The police report was clean and, if the Innocence Project accused him of misconduct, he'd just respond that the allegation was ridiculous. Case closed. There had to be some way to get Phil to keep his mouth shut; but for now, all he could do was hope things never came down to Phil.

The alternative, working on the Innocence Project, was no better. If their work is leading to Doug, the Project must suspect something close to the truth. Calling Glassman, then, would be a mistake. It would only increase their interest in him.

Then again, maybe he was wrong about Doug. Maybe Doug had nothing to do with the stranglings and the whole Apache Tear gambit was unnecessary. If so, it was wrong; but what harm did it do other than increase the pressure to convict Swenson of a murder of which he was undoubtedly guilty. The fact that the stranglings stopped when Dougie was moved out of the City might be no more meaningful than the fact that they stopped when Swenson himself was incarcerated. The real strangler may have relocated to Chicago or some other safer place. This happy thought relieved the tightness in his stomach for a few seconds until he remembered the strangling of Carl Watson's wife on the same road as Dougie's trailer park, at about the same time Dougie left the area. Of course that too could be coincidence, particularly since Carl's wife was so much younger than the Strangler's other victims. But as he thought about it, the tightness returned.

He sat sphinx-like for minutes before Elizabeth entered with a barrage of questions about Zapo and his family. The interruption had John breathing deeply through his nose and he couldn't disguise his eagerness to get back to his thoughts.

"Okay, John," said Elizabeth. "I'll leave you alone. Looks like Zapo had some bad news. Hope he's not ill."

Ranzone waived his wife away, hoping he could use Carl Watson's death as an excuse for his surliness when he finished making his plans.

In time, a plan of sorts emerged. To start, he'd have to find out the name of the Innocence Project staffer who had been poking around. No doubt, Father Bill had put him on to Zapo. So he called the St. Francis rectory and asked for Monsignor Ranzone.

When Father Bill took the call, John started in without any hello-how-are-yous.

"Bill? John here. I got a call from Zapo a few minutes ago. To wish me well on the campaign. But he mentioned someone was asking him about Dougie. You know anything about that?" He assumed Father Bill would remember that visit from the Innocence Project; but didn't mention it by name. "Not that we wouldn't want to find Dougie, but he could be an embarrassment for the campaign."

Father Bill said he understood and told John about the young man from the Innocence project. Owen Delaney was his name. Pleasant chap. Striking blond hair, maybe forty years old. The call did not take long but John hung up breathing more slowly now that he had the name of his antagonist. Although forty seemed old to be volunteering for the Innocence Project.

So, what to do next? Should he hunt for Dougie? Or try to stop Delaney? Stopping Delaney would be helpful only if Delaney hadn't shared any information with the Innocence Project. And that was unlikely. So it made more sense to hunt Dougie down himself. If he found Doug before Delaney, Dougie could be moved again. If Dougie couldn't be found, that might be good news, even though he hated to think of Dougie as dead or homeless. Failing Doug was still a source of pain for John. His only fear was that Delaney would find Doug first.

Ranzone knew that searching for Dougie himself was an impossibility. The election was only days away. He couldn't just disappear to Florida. He'd need to find someone, a good Florida detective, say, to do the job. And he'd have to keep the search under wraps, probably even going so far as to have someone else find the detective for him. Phil Conry would be the obvious choice; but that could get complicated down the road if Phil was ever questioned about that Apache Tear. Not only that, but he doubted Phil knew anyone down in Florida.

Ranzone tapped his foot wildly as he scrambled to remember anyone he knew in Florida who might find a decent detective, until he came up with the obvious choice: Michael Calderone. He recalled that Calderone had retired to a place in Florida called the Villages, near Orlando. Calderone still owed him and would surely keep the engagement secret. Not only that, but he certainly didn't have to know the true story. John could tell him he was worried about an eleventh hour scandal over Doug and he wanted to find Doug to prepare the campaign for that possibility. And, knowing Calderone, he would still be shady enough to know the right person for the job. And, knowing Calderone, that right person could deal with Delaney should that become necessary.

The next day Ranzone had a clerk in the DA's office find the cell phone number for retired Lt. Detective Michael Calderone in Florida. He called from his room in the Scranton LaQuinta where he'd asked for some privacy to work on the speech he was to give to a Rotary Club luncheon that afternoon. When Calderone answered, he claimed to have a hard time hearing John.

"I'm in my golf cart, John. The street's packed with them today."

"The street?"

"Yeah. Great place, the Villages. Drive around town in a golf cart. It's legal. And for an old divorced cop like me, the sex is great."

"What?"

"This place is like a college campus in the seventies. No fear of pregnancy, so anything goes. Highest rates of STDs of any senior living community in the nation. And highest averge credit scores. Doesn't that tell ya all ya gotta know. And some of these old divorcees ain't bad."

Ranzone remembered all the things he'd hated about Calderone; but pressed on.

"Mike, I didn't just call to hear abut your sex life. I need a favor."

Ranzone explained the need to find his derelict brother before the press or his campaign opponent did, the need to prevent an irrelevant scandal, the need for a forceful private detective. Calderone understood and put John on hold, to park his cart and check something, he said. It took maybe forty seconds.

"John, I think I got the perfect guy. Curt Shapiro. Ex-cop from New York. Met him at one of the pools. Interesting story. Apparently, as a beat cop he did some good police work for a biggie in the City Housing Department. The guy wanted to reward him and Shapiro asked what up and coming areas would be good for real estate investments. He and some friends were thinking of buying a few small properties. The biggie gave him advice about planned urban renewal projects and the rest is history. The properties were beat up but he developed what he called special skills dealing with the problem tenants. And when time came to move them out to avoid rent control and take advantage of a rising market, he was, shall we say, very persuasive. His little syndicate did this over and over until he had a sweet little nest egg, retired after twenty, still a young guy, and came down here to the Villages to enjoy the good life. But he got himself a license and does some work on the side. All around the state. He's got a unique reputation."

Shapiro sounded like the kind of guy Ranzone needed, particularly if Delaney got ahead in the hunt for Dougie. So he took Shapiro's number and asked Calderone to let the detective know to expect a call.

Chapter 20

I.D. Pinkett gave his first report to Owen two days after Owen called him. In the interim, Owen had done nothing on the Swenson/Dougie Ranzone matter but worry whether or not he should do anything at all. Within the blink of an eye, it had become a lot more than an academic exercise. And he was uncomfortable with the idea that, if he pushed forward, he'd end up needing to travel to Florida. Although he could concoct some believable rationale why his academic exercise would require him to go, anything near the truth would probably alarm Barbara. So he was ambivalent when he received I.D.'s call.

Apparently, there was an old geezer at the Bel Aire who remembered Doug. As he recalled, Doug had left suddenly. Sold his trailer and drove off in his old pick-up. The trailer was still in the park, owned by the very guy who had bought it from Doug, an eighty-year-old named McLoughlin. I.D. found him sitting under a canopy attached to the rusted trailer. All McLoughlin remembered was that Doug said he was moving to the Tampa area. To live with a couple of friends.

I.D asked if Doug had left a forwarding address. According to I.D., when asked that same question, McLoughlin squinted and struggled in his walker to the trailer door. Turning back toward I.D. before wrenching himself up the two steps to the door, he pointed an index finger in the air, giving I.D. some hope that he'd find something. But he limped out of the trailer after about five minutes shaking his head. He had found nothing. I.D. wrote out his number on a scrap of paper—worried that it didn't look sufficiently official—asked McLoughlin to call if he found anything, and left. Disappointed.

I.D.'s detailed account of his disappointment was a little out of character. Owen would have expected it to have been more matter-of-fact. But I.D.'s dramatics were apparently just intended to lay the groundwork for his rabbit pulling. He must have enjoyed going back to his old trade. Surprisingly, he *did* get a call from McLoughlin. The old guy had found the names and address of Dougie's Tampa friends to whom McLoughlin had forwarded Dougie's mail for a few weeks. Apparently Doug had not made arrangements with the postal service. I.D gave the names and address to Owen. No phone number.

PeopleSearch was very helpful this time. Both friends were still listed at the old address, with a phone number that turned out to be an active landline. Owen called and asked for Dan Lundy, the first name I.D. had given him. The weak voice that answered acknowledged he was Dan Lundy. But when Owen said he was looking for Doug Ranzone, Lundy said he'd never heard of him.

"Are you sure, Mr. Lundy? I was told he left Sarasota in the late 90s to move in with you and a Mr. Ted Boyle. Sure you don't remember him?"

"Hold on a sec." Lundy's voice muted a bit but Owen could still understand him as he spoke to someone else nearby. "Ted, you remember a guy named Ranzone? Supposedly stayed with us in the late 90s?" Owen could not hear Ted's response, but in a few seconds Lundy said "Here, talk to my roommate."

"Hello? You looking for Doug Ranzone?"

"Right. Do you remember him?"

"Yeah. Danny's memory ain't too good. And we always need help with the rent so we take in a third roomie every once in a while. Even I can't remember all of 'em. But I'm pretty sure the guy we met at a bar in Sarasota was named Doug Ranzone. We was down there for a Reds spring training game and after the game went to a noisy bar on the main street in town. Met this guy who said he needed to move to Tampa. Danny and I invited him to stay with us. I'm pretty sure his name was Doug."

"Obviously, he's not still living there."

"No. He moved out after maybe two years and we ain't seen him since. Said he was afraid of the neighborhood."

"Afraid?"

"Yeah, there was some killings around here and he was scared. I'm pretty sure he said he was headed for Miami."

"Miami?" Owen puffed up his cheeks and blew a long breath that was obviously too loud.

"Right. Crazy, ain't it? Miami! As though that's safer than here. Our neighborhood wasn't that bad; and them killings was all older women. Don't know why Ranzone was scared for himself. But as I say, that was the last we seen or heard of 'em."

Owen thought he could actually feel the hairs on his neck stand on end. "No forwarding address, I assume."

"You kiddin me? He had no idea where he'd land, Maybe never even got to Miami."

Owen let all the information sink in. Those Tampa stranglings certainly fed his worse fears about Doug and he had to remind himself that he did indeed have flights of fancy, as Kopinski had called them. But incriminating or not, the update on the Dougie Ranzone story sure made it less likely that Owen would ever find him.

Chapter 21

Curt Shapiro was in bed with a slightly older woman when Ranzone called. It was one-thirty in the afternoon and it was not too unusual for Shapiro to have found a widow or divorcee to bed by that time. He'd told all his New York friends the truth. The pools scattered around the Villages were like singles bars of his youth. Same games, same women, just older. Being only fifty-two, he was a little younger than most of the women, though some of them were in better shape than he was. This Gloria he was with was a yoga instructor, for God's sake.

Shapiro pulled on his swim-suit, told Gloria he had to take the call outside, stepped on to the balcony off her pink and white bedroom and slid the heavy glass door closed behind him. He never brought women to his place because too much about him became obvious once you went in there. Poor housekeeper, no food in the frig, signs of regular drinking. And maybe a handgun sitting on a bureau or coffee table. He couldn't be bothered to keep it all up for guests. Especially when his women were so anxious to show him the sweet little nests they had made for themselves.

The chat with Ranzone was short and sweet. Mike Calderon had filled him in on the basics and Ranzone pointed him in the only direction he could, the Belmont or Bell Meade trailer park on 41 between Bradenton and Sarasota. They agreed on rates and careful methods of communication; and Ranzone reminded him that the election was only a week away, so time was of the essence.

When the call ended, Shapiro sat on a wicker chair on the balcony and stared at the man-made lake squirming, amoeba-like, through the clusters of town homes that comprised Gloria's area of the Villages. It passed about fifty yards behind Gloria's townhouse. On the far side of the lake was a golf course, nearly empty in the afternoon heat. He studied a single in green shorts and a pink shirt hurrying through his round and then noticed a good sized alligator sunning himself on the sloped water's edge, Gloria's side. So still. Could have been a huge rock.

Alligators fascinated him. He'd been told that they would walk miles to find a new aquatic hunting ground when they had depleted their old lake or pond of turtles, fish and birds. How the hell did they find the new water? Could they smell it? Or just sense it. Animal instinct. Sometimes he though of himself as having uncommon instincts too. And what he was sniffing just then was a financial bonanza. If that pissant housing guy in the City was able to help him make a small fortune, what could a governor do for him? Particularly now that he had some real money to invest. Maybe Ranzone's story about heading off a scandal about his brother's drinking made some sense. But it felt like there was more to it. Otherwise why all the secrecy? Why Calderone? Mike had said that Ranzone and he went way back. But from the stories Mike had shared, way back for Mike was a pretty dark place. A good job for the guv had to be worth something big. But he'd said time was of the essence.

Shapiro went back inside, yanked on his tee shirt, slipped on his sandals, told Gloria he had to go, and quickstepped out to his golf cart and drove home.

Chapter 22

Owen's indecision exhausted him. While the news about the stranglings that preceeded Dougie's sudden moves down in Florida was persuading him that his suspicions about John Ranzone were correct, he couldn't kid himself into thinking he could find Doug in Miami without any leads. That is, if Doug ever made it to Miami. That is, if Doug were still even alive. And even if he found him, wasn't it a little much to think he'd be able to know from talking to Doug whether he was the Strangler or not? He had spent hours toying with his go/no go decision before his do-gooder instincts prevailed and he decided he owed it to himself and, more grandiosely, to the Commonwealth of Pennsylvania, to do the best he could. He then tried out different ideas on how to find Doug. None excited him. So he called Geoff Shultz in the evening and filled him in on the latest developments.

"I see you have yourself a problem, old boy." Geoff sometimes liked to sound old school professorial and, this time, it pissed Owen off.

"Well, why do you think I called you, old boy?" Owen tone was sharper than he had intended.

"Okay. Okay," Shultz said and then went silent for a few seconds. "Let's think this through."

"That's what I've been doing all day."

"And?"

"Well . . ." Owen began with the working assumption that, if still alive, Doug had remained in Florida. Shultz agreed that was a reasonable start. But Owen reminded Shultz that the *PeopleSearch* work he'd done when they were last together had come up with nothing useful.

"Yeah. But I'd guess you could search public records yourself. That website could be out of date. Or incomplete."

"Where would you look?"

"I'd try motor vehicle records, maybe criminal histories. I know they're accessible. Civil court records as well."

Owen's pulse quickened. Why hadn't he thought of that? He'd become a slave to that *PeopleSearch* site, is why. He shook his head as his mind raced, searching for other possibilities.

"His brother's a politician. It wouldn't surprise me if Doug voted at least once since leaving Tampa. Voter records might show that. And if they did, they'd have to give an address for Doug."

"Good," Shultz said, "maybe." He paused, mumbled, and Owen could just see him bouncing his head in indecision. "Don't know how many semi-retarded alcoholics vote. And are Florida voter registrations open to the public?"

"Don't know. But that should be easy enough to find out." Owen said, then took a deep breath and said he should get started right away.

Two hours later, after pecking away at his computer, calling up all sorts of websites purporting to have information of the sort he was after, Owen's pulse had slowed considerably. Most of the websites had nothing. No obituaries. No judgments. Others required information he didn't know: driver's license number for driving records; some sort of document number or other identification for court based records or real estate filings. Date of death for death certificates. Birthdate for voter registration. It was nearly ten o'clock and Barb had been reading in the family room since the kids had gone to bed. He thought sitting with her for a while might cheer him up, so he left his office and plodded into the family room. Barbara immediately saw his mood.

"What's up, hon? You look like you have the weight of the world on your shoulders."

Owen was reluctant to go into details, wary that the full story about John Ranzone would alarm Barb. But he did say that he was unable to locate someone In Florida he wanted to interview for the Swenson case.

"Florida? How is someone from Florida involved in that Swenson case?"

"Moved. And *PeopleSearch* was no help. If only I had his birthdate, I might be able to find something in the voter registration records. But I haven't got a clue."

" You can't look that up?"

"Nope. He's not a public figure. Can't find records for him anywhere."

"Is there anyone who might know it?"

"Can't think of anyone to ask." Owen slouched and grabbed the TV remote. "Mind if I watch something?"

"No go ahead, I'm getting sleepy anyway."

Barb went upstairs and Owen watched the replay of a college football game. Notre Dame vs Purdue. At halftime, a sideline reporter interviewed the Notre Dame team chaplain about a minor player scandal that had upset the team during the previous week. The soft face and reassuring voice of the chaplain reminded Owen of Father Bill, and it occurred to him that Father

Bill would know Dougie's birthday. He decided to call him first thing in the morning, hoping that a third conversation with Father Bill would not raise awkward questions within the Ranzone family.

Owen reached Father Bill early, just as he returned to his rectory from saying the eight o'clock mass at St. Francis. Owen explained that he hadn't found Dougie yet, but he might have better luck with public records if he knew Doug's birthdate. Father Bill knew it by heart, gave it to Owen hurriedly and said he had another religion class to teach in the grade school and had to go. Owen's pulse quickened again and he searched once more for the Florida voter registration site that had frustrated him the previous evening.

Bingo! Plugging Doug's full name and birthdate into the Florida Voter Registration archive site gave Owen an address in Miami, Dade County. Further research indicated the address was in the Bayshore area of Miami Beach.

Just wondering, he searched the address in google-maps and was shown a picture of a church. Bayshore Community Church. He tried again. Same picture. Found the street level scan and went up and down the block. Low rise apartments, parking lot and the church at the corner. He got the phone number from the church website and called.

A reverend Garcia with a thick Hispanic accent took Owen's call and explained that one of the church's missions was to serve as a resource center for the homeless. Apparently, there were a surprising number of homeless in Miami Beach because it was safer and more affluent than other more blighted areas of the city. And one of the services the church offered was an address for the homeless to use for mail and other identification purposes. And yes, sometimes homeless from the area used the church as their address for voter registration. There was a voting place two blocks from the church and registering the church as their address put homeless on the voting rolls in that precinct. One of the junior clerics had been very aggressive registering voters from the area; but he'd left the ministry for more politically active work on the Gulf Coast about five years earlier.

"Do you have any information about the homeless who've used your address?"

"I'm sure there's some kind of book around but it hasn't been maintained very well since Reverend Clarke left." Garcia paused before offering to look for it. "Call me back tomorrow morning. I should be able to find it by then. What was the name you were looking for?"

"Douglas Ranzone." Owen pinched his shoulders in anticipation of closing in on Doug. He spelled out the name slowly. "I'd appreciate any help you can give me. His family's been looking for him for years." That last bit may or may not've been true. Owen didn't know; but chalked it up as another half-lie that had to be told for the cause.

"Bueno." Said Reverend Garcia. "I'll see what we have on him."

Chapter 23

Shapiro thought the communication protocol Ranzome had set up was unnecessarily cautious and cumbersome. But within two hours after calling an answering service and leaving a message for John Rogers, he got a return call. Ranzone called from a motel room, using a phone Ranzone said was untraceable, bought for him at a Dollar Store by a campaign aide.

"What've you found? Anything good?" Ranzone spoke at just above a whisper.

"I don't think it's good. I've made some progress. Tracked him from Bradenton to Tampa. But he left Tampa about fifteen years ago, supposedly for Miami, afraid of Tampa because some women had been strangled in his neighborhood. Miami address unknown. Yet. But the bad news is I'm not the only one looking for him. There's an old, black, plainclothes cop a little ahead of me."

Shapiro paused, curious how Ranzone would react to that news. When he himself learned it, it only confirmed that there was more to this Dougie problem than a potential scandal about an alcoholic brother. If not, why would a cop be looking for him too? What could Doug have done? How much more would solving this problem for the would-be governor be worth?

Ranzone felt like someone had reached into his chest and squeezed his heart. A detective was one thing; but why a cop looking for Dougie? Was Dougie a suspect in the strangling of Carl Watson's wife. Or those Tampa stranglings? Or others?

There was no way the Philadelphia Innocence Project would engage the police. And no way the police would respond if they'd tried. It's not their job to prove someone innocent. Not only that, but Father Bill had said the guy from the Innocence Project was about forty with very blond hair—he couldn't remember his name—not old and black. What ever happened to him? What was he doing about Dougie? He asked Shapiro to hold on.

It took Ranzone almost five minutes of sorting through two briefcases to find the scrap on which he'd scribbled the name of the Innocence Project visitor to Father Bill. Owen Delaney.

"Listen. You have any contacts in Philly?"

"Sure, plenty."

"Okay. Get your best to track down a guy named Owen Delaney. Don't know anything about him other than he's, say, forty years old and has very blond hair."

"I can do that; but do you want me to keep going down here? I was thinking of doing some digging in Miami."

"Yes. Keep looking for Doug. Miami's a big place; but if he's there, there's got to be a record of him somewhere."

"Fine. I'll drive down there today."

"Wouldn't flying be faster? We've only got a few days."

"Not really. By the time I find a flight—whenever that turns out to be—get to the airport, wait for the plane, and rent a car at the other end, I could be there already. It's only a four hour drive; and it'll be much cheaper."

Saving money was fine with Ranzone. Those Philly private eyes would add to his costs and he wasn't a rich man. Though his mortgage was just about paid off and he could look forward to a decent pension, with two kids put through college and now helping with tuitions for three grandkids, he had not saved much of his civil servants salary over the years. He wondered if all this stuff was a legitimate campaign expense. He would have suggested that Phil Conry look into it if Phil wasn't in a position to guess the truth about Dougie. Damn that Phil. If he'd just kept his mouth shut about that Apache Tear, there would be no Dougie problem, no expense. Phil's stupidity—or was it just reflexive honesty—made his chest tighten. He didn't feel well and had to force himself to relax and breathe easy.

Shapiro called a detective firm in Philly that he'd engaged before and asked them to put as many men as needed to find the Owen Delaney Ranzone had described. He gave no reason for the search; but agreed on a fee and waited. It did not take long. There were only two fortyish Owen Delaneys in Philly and the surrounding area. One detective had been assigned to each and, by four o'clock that afternoon, they had a report that the blond one had been spotted in Chestnut Hill greeting his kids as they got off their school bus. Per Ranzone's instructions, Shapiro ordered the Philly group to trail that Delaney twenty-four-seven.

Chapter 24

Owen's stomach was churning. Little Hank said he needed more help with his new math and, though Owen generally loved working with the earnest boy, he had been wrestling with his own kind of new math when the school bus arrived. He wanted to continue thinking through the pros and con's of a trip to Miami, whether Reverend Garcia had information about Dougie or not. If he did and it was useful, he'd have no hesitation about flying down there except for the mild deception of Barb that the trip would require. But if Reverend Garcia could not add anything more than the fact that Doug had used the church as a voter registration address, the decision became more difficult. While that registration would undoubtedly mean that Doug had been hanging around the area where the church was located, there was no knowing if he was still there. The Reverend Clarke had left the church five years before, so that meant Doug had probably been registered at least that many years ago. Was he still in the neighborhood? And if he were, how would Owen actually find him. He didn't even have a picture.

But more to the point was the question of what he could really learn from Doug. If he found Doug, and Doug was in fact the Strangler, Doug certainly wasn't going to purge his guilt with a gushing confession to a complete stranger. Geoff Shultz's suggestion that Owen would know the state of Doug's soul by talking to him seemed even more painfully presumptuous than it had when he started looking for Doug, now that an actual meeting with Doug was a possibility.

Owen's tension grew as the math session with Little Hank dragged on for almost two hours and, with dinner and bedtime, it was not until almost nine when Owen went back to his deliberations. Sitting almost motionless at his office desk for what seemed like forever, he once again came down on the side of making the noble try, regardless of what Reverend Garcia had to offer. If he didn't find Doug, so be it. If he found him and learned nothing definitive, at least he'd tried. And if he found him and Doug unexpectedly confessed or implied guilt in some other way, he would do something about it. Exactly what, he wasn't sure.

On the other hand, as he emerged from his near stupor, it occurred to Owen that Dougie's registration could be stale, even more than five years old, depending on how long that Reverend Clarke had been dong his good work. He could have left Miami anytime since he initially registered to vote.

So he clicked on his desktop and went back to the Florida Voter Registration site to check the rules for keeping a voter on the registration rolls. He exhaled slowly when he read that, unless a voter asks to be dropped, he or she cannot be dropped unless they have failed to vote in two successive general elections. Since Doug was still on the rolls, that would mean he had voted in the general election two years prior, or at most four years ago. That closed the window a bit.

Owen made an online reservation on a late morning flight to Miami for the next day and a motel reservation in the Bayshore area. He then went in to the family room where Barb was watching a replay of her Sunday Masterpiece Theater and told her he'd probably found that person of interest in the Swenson case and would be flying to Miami to interview him. Not sure how long it would take. He was tempted to tell her the full truth because he was certain Doug, if found, would be a fragile and homeless old man; and certain that neither Conry nor Ranzone had any idea he was still working the Swenson case. But he didn't tell Barb the truth.

The next morning before taking the Chestnut Hill Local to Thirtieth Street Station and the SEPTA Airport line to Philadelphia International, he called Reverend Garcia and learned that the Bayshore Community Church records had no information on Douglas Ranzone other than he had been registered to vote in the year before Reverend Clarke left the area.

Too bad; but so what.

Chapter 25

Shapiro was the last guest eating at the Holiday Inn breakfast buffet when he received a call about ten am from the Philadelphia man trailing Owen. He had followed Owen on public transportation to the airport where he exited the Airport Line at the American Airlines terminal. The tail had maneuvered himself behind Delaney at the check-in kiosk and, best he could tell, saw that Delaney was booked on a flight to Miami. He couldn't get by security to follow Delaney to his gate, but from the flight board, he guessed Delaney was taking the eleven-thirty. He suggested that Shapiro pick him up at the Miami end.

"You can't miss 'em. Wearing a tweed sport coat and khakis. Carrying a leather briefcase and an overnight bag and has the most amazing blond hair you ever seen."

The job didn't sound particularly easy to Shapiro. Delaney had several travel options leaving the Miami airport. He could take a cab, rent a car or even take public transportation. If he took a cab or public transportation, tailing him would be relatively easy. Get on the same bus or grab the next taxi to follow him. But if he'd rented a car, how could he follow him. Car rentals agencies were a bus ride from the Arrival exits. He could hop on the Avis bus or Budget bus or whatever bus Delaney took. But that would mean he'd have to rent a car at the same agency and hope he could get through the paperwork fast enough to stick with Delaney. And that would mean he'd either have to take public transportation to the Airport or leave his own car behind when he rented one to trail Delaney.

He realized he needed help. Though still hungry, he dumped this breakfast in the trash slot, put his plastic tray on the return pile and hurried back to his room, mentally running through a list of ex-cops he knew in Miami. Just as the elevator pinged its stop at his floor, he thought of Billy Garrity. Garrity had been more traditional in his retirement move: to Miami where he could indulge his passion for fishing. He and Bill had talked several times about a visit to Miami for a charter boat excursion. Once inside his room, Shapiro sat at the edge of his bed and called. When Bill answered, Shapiro didn't want to get sidetracked with fishing stories, so he rushed to the point.

"Hey Bill, this is Curt. I need your help on something at the Airport. You free?"

"I guess so. Was gonna do some bone-fishing in the Biscayne flats this afternoon. But I can adjust. This a paid gig?"

"Sure, but it shouldn't take too long. You might even be able to do that fishing later."

Shapiro explained that he needed a second pair of eyes to lock onto a target arriving from Phiiladelphia on the America flight arriving from Philadelphia at about 2:30 pm. The guy would be easy to spot as he came off the American concourse; and he wanted Billy to follow him to the street and phone him with Delaney's next steps. If he took a cab, get the next one and follow him, directing Shapiro by cell phone as they went so that he could catch up in his car. Same with a bus. If he left for a car rental agency, go with him and let Shapiro know where he was headed. If there was a hard part, it would start there. Billy had to somehow identify the car Delaney had rented so Curt could pick it up as he left the agency. God knows a lot of those cars will look the same.

"You're right. It's gets tricky if he rents a car. But if I stick near him at the rental counter, I might be able to get some information about what he'll be driving." Garrity made a sucking sound that Shapiro interpreted as indecision, particularly when Garrity said "Who is this guy, anyway?"

"I think he's a reporter, trying to dig up some dirt on my client's brother. The client's a public figure and the brother's an alcoholic, he says. I think the brother's here in Miami and this Delaney might know where he is. My job is to prevent that story from coming out."

"How exactly you gonna do that?"

"Find the brother first and get him outta here."

"And suppose that Delaney knows where the brother is and goes straight to him for the story? Wha'dya do then?"

"Not sure, but I'll figure it out. All I need you for is to help me pick him up when he leaves the airport. You in?"

"Guess so. Give me that information again."

Shapiro gave Garrity a description of Delaney and his flight information, told him to call at least every ten minutes once Delaney's plane touched down and, finally, agreed on Garrity's fee. It was about eleven and, if the Philly guy was correct, Delaney's flight should arrive In Miami at about two-thirty. He checked out of the Holiday Inn and drove to the airport, stopping to resume his breakfast at a Taco Bell on the way.

Chapter 26

Owen had no clue that he was being followed. Had he thought about it, though, he would have realized that his quick pace down the concourse to the street would have made him noticeable to anyone looking for him, the blond, academic-looking, forty-year old racing through the terminal to the waiting area for the bus to Budget Rentals.

Owen was uncomfortable in his tweed sport coat and slipped it off and draped it over his overnight bag, which he'd set on the curb. He took a deep breath, sucking in the warm, moist Miami air with satisfaction. October in Miami was like August in Philly. The almost tropical day moved the needle a bit on his cheer meter and, somehow, his decision to pursue Dougie now seemed completely sensible and the right thing to do.

The bus to the rental agency was air-conditioned and almost empty. Had he not been ruminating about his next steps, he might have noticed that one of the other passengers, the only one with no luggage, was staring at him periodically. And he might have noticed that, on stepping off the bus at Budget, that bulky older man had followed close behind him into the rental office and stuck with him as he approached the rental agent who waved Owen toward her. He had stood in line behind Owen even though there were two free agents further along the counter.

Owen paid little attention to the paperwork which had a boldly written parking space identified in red; but when the agent gave him his packet of rental papers, he did ask her directions for Miami Beach, specifically an area called Bayshore. She was very helpful, unfolding a map of Miami and tracing the best route with the same red magic marker. Engrossed, Owen did not notice that, after peeking at the papers on the counter, the bulky man had stepped back, out of earshot, and make a phone call while looking at Owen all the while.

Shapiro ignored a few one-way signs guiding the Budget renters away from their exit kiosk; and idled in an alcove with a good view of exiting drivers, waiting for the green Honda Garrity had identified when he followed Owen. He noticed Owen's hair immediately; and expertly glided in behind him and trailed him from the airport on NW 42nd Avenue to Interstate 195 and across Biscayne Bay to Miami Beach. There, Delaney turned south and confidently made numerous turns before pulling up to an older motel called the Bayshore Inn. Either he had been there before or his GPS gave very clear instructions. Shapiro parked at a fire hydrant, called John Rogers' answering service and waited. It took Ranzone almost an hour to call back. But fortunately, Delaney had remained in the motel the whole time. When Shapiro's phone rang it was already in his hand, which he was tapping unconsciously on the console.

"John, I've got Delaney. He's in a motel on Miami Beach. You think he's meeting your brother in there?"

Ranzone said nothing and after a pause that worried Shapiro, Shapiro asked again "You think he's meeting your brother in there?"

"Hope not. If he is, we're screwed. Any way you can check?"

"I could try; but I don't want to spook him. Why don't I just sit here until something happens. What does your brother look like?"

"I have no idea what he would look like now. He's fifty-nine and I haven't seen him since he was in his thirties. But he was never a very big guy; and frankly, he always had the look of someone who wasn't completely with it."

"Okay. Suppose I see him come out. What then?"

"Grab him and tell him his brother John wants to talk. Call me and hold on to him till I call back."

"And what if he doesn't come out. If Delaney hasn't met with him yet?"

"Then follow Delaney and don't let him find Dougie." Ranzone gave a heavy sigh. "Unless of course, you can find Dougie first. But it seems like Delaney at least has something to go on. Why else would he go to a specific neighborhood?" Ranzone sighed again. "You have any idea why he's there? In this Bayshore place, I mean?"

"Nope, but it does seem like he's one step ahead. If I go off trying to find your brother, I'd miss whatever Delaney's up to. And he's probably on to something."

"Maybe."

"Not just maybe, sir. Even if he finds your brother, I can probably persuade him not to do the article he's hopin' to write. I've done that before." Shapiro was thinking of the time a Daily News reporter wanted to do an article on his housing operation. His self-help tactics and his forcing tenants out of rent controlled units. But a little roughing up made the reporter less interested in his expose.

"What did you do?"

"Well, I have special skills when it comes to persuasion."

"Don't tell me any more about it. Please."

"Sure thing. Guv."

Chapter 27

The conversation with Shapiro had not comforted John Ranzone one bit. On the contrary, within seconds of hanging up he felt a heavy pressure in his chest, like two unseen hands pinning him against a wall. Breathing was difficult. Sure Shapiro's special persuasion skills might work on a reporter with nothing at stake but a good story. But Delaney was after something bigger. He wasn't even certain what Shapiro had meant by special persuasion skills. How far did they go? It all reminded him of the day he'd shown that Apache Tear to Phil Conry. Though he'd managed to suppress the Apache Tear anxiety from time to time, he knew back then he was, for want of a better phrase, committing a serious sin; that he was starting down a path with no return. He was afraid he might be doing the same thing with this guy Shapiro.

Ranzone had made the call from the campaign limo parked outside a restaurant where the others had gone for lunch. He'd told them he'd join them after he made a few calls; but lost his appetite after speaking with Shapiro. And he wasn't up to any campaign planning. Or gloating. What he craved was someone to talk to about the Swenson mess, someone who'd tell him that it wasn't that big a deal. Someone to absolve him of the fear and guilt, to help put it behind that door for good. Like the priests to whom he confessed his sins as a boy. Unlike most of his friends, he actually liked confession. At least until he went away to college and fell away from his religious habits. He'd always been one to wrestle endlessly with guilt. He had not been able to be in the same room with his father for days after sneaking that first summer beer at the playground when he was thirteen. And, once he knew she wasn't pregnant, he never spoke again to Sandra what-was-her-name after they'd had sex in the back of the family Plymouth the night of the junior prom. Confession always made him feel better about those kind of things. But that kind of stuff was nothing. Catholic kid's stuff. When it threatened to push open that door to the secret basement, the Swenson case triggered industrial strength fear and guilt. He could beat it back; but couldn't get it to die. Like those horrible dreams as a grade schooler, in which he protected his family from intruders with his baseball bat. Every time he put one away, another came flying at him until he woke up exhausted and soaked with sweat. Or like those kung-foo movies where the hero holds off a never-ending assault of kicks and karate chops from an army of barefoot warriors in loose black outfits.

He told himself he'd only been trying to help his baby brother. For his parents' sake. It wasn't some selfishly ambitious move to advance his career. And, he was sure he'd never have done it if he wasn't convinced Swenson was guilty. And, he had to remind himself for the millionth time, that the fact the stranglings stopped after Dougie left Philly could have been a coincidence. With any luck, after he'd moved Dougie, Dougie would have lived an okay life. That was all he'd hoped for when he asked Zapo and Carl to watch out for him. But now that he was on the verge of the big payoff for his hard work and ambition, his rationalizations felt weak. Twenty plus years of keeping his full weight against the door to the secret basement was wearing him out.

He scratched the back of one hand mindlessly. Though he felt stupid talking to himself in metaphors, he told himself that what he needed was a permanent lock on the door so he could go about his business with no fear of its being forced open. He was kidding himself if he thought some sort of confession would wash away the dread. What he needed was to eliminate the possibility of disclosure. Even if the Innocence Project got nowhere, their poking around could be just the opening shot. Who knows who else might get suspicious? He leaned his head back and closed his eyes. Damn, he was tired.

Chapter 28

Owen called the Reverend Garcia immediately after settling in his motel room. Garcia was meeting with a paving contractor about resurfacing the church parking lot; and he didn't get back to Owen for half an hour. When he called back, Garcia gave Owen a list of places where the homeless of the area congregated: the local library branch, a small city park, a Salvation Army shelter and a cheap rooming house where some of them stayed when they had money. Owen marked the spots as best he could on the map he had been given at the car rental check-in; and then stretched out on his bed to rest before hitting the streets. Almost against his will, he slept for an hour.

When he awoke, it was four pm. He massaged his face with cold water, patted it dry and grabbed his map. Checking the map, he realized he might be better off walking to the homeless hangouts Garcia had described. They weren't that far away or that far apart and walking might cross his path with other homeless he could question. So he headed first for the library, just in case it closed early.

He did pass one obviously homeless woman pushing a Publix shopping cart stuffed with bags of clothes that smelled like the moldy areas of the basement of his one hundred year old stone house in Chestnut Hill. He asked her if she knew a Douglas Ranzone. She didn't answer other than with a wave of her hand in front of her face and a shake of her head. Without saying a word, she plodded off in her slippers and long coat. It occurred to him he should've just asked for Doug or Dougie.

The library was a one-story brick building with assorted benches bordering a wide concrete entry apron. The benches were full with men, for the most part, with a knapsack or bag of one sort or another at their feet. The bags and knapsacks were to be expected, he supposed. But he was surprised at how well some of the men were turned out. Maybe most needed a haircut; but their clothes fit reasonable well and were more or less appropriate. Replica Miami Dolphin uniform tops with blue jeans, Bermudas and tee shirts, even a few wrinkled Tommy Bahama short-sleeved prints. No overly warm outfits like the ones he'd see in Philadelphia or on that woman he'd just met. He moved from bench to bench, asking about Doug, or Dougie or Douglas. The name met with blank stares from everyone. But the few women in the crowd, all of whom were less put together than the men, were eager to engage in conversation, as though being helpful to a stranger made them feel like actual residents of the area. And maybe, Owen thought, it was fair to consider them just that.

After finishing his circuit of the outside benches, Owen went inside the library. It was air conditioned, so it was not surprising that many of what appeared to be the homeless were there, reading at library tables with apparent studiousness. Owen noticed a security guard hovering and decided he'd be unable to engage in prolonged conversation with them inside the library. He left.

Outside, he checked his map and decided to head for the city park, which was the destination closest to the library. Garcia said it was a pocket park so it should not be too extensive an area to cover. It was four blocks away.

The park was not much more than a fenced-in, corner lot. A bronze plaque at its entrance dedicated it to the memory of some local politician named Caruso who had lived in the area. A curved gravel walkway went from a gated entrance to a gated exit on the intersecting side street. The walkway was lined with wrought iron benches. There was grass, yellowed by dog pee. The doggy clean-up-bag dispensers were empty.

All the benches were full, with several men or woman at each bench standing around unable to find a seat. Bicycles had been flopped down here and there and, as at the library, belongings were always nearby, in a black plastic bag or tired knapsack. While there were a couple of neighborhood women walking dogs (and carrying their own clean up bags, thank God), the park seemed to have been more permanently colonized by homeless than the library. There was more shouting and laughter and some sleeping along the fence away from the noisy walkway benches.

Owen strolled into the park to the first pair of benches and asked the crowds on each side of the gravel path whether they knew anyone by the name of Doug, or Dougie, or Douglas. They all denied knowing anyone by that name and they all, including the women, inspected Owen with a faint animosity he hadn't felt at the library. None seemed to feel even the slightest sense of importance that a civilian had paid a vist to their little commune. So Owen moved on, from bench to bench until he arrived at the park exit. No luck at any stop. In fact, the short walk had actually scared him a bit. The men were aggressive in asking him for money and he worried that some of them were sizing him up for a mugging. He was happy to move on to the cheap flophouse.

When Shapiro saw Owen leave his motel on foot, he had no choice but to leave his car in front of the fire hydrant and follow. He stayed a half block behind and then watched from across the street while Owen chatted with the homeless people at the library. When Owen went inside, he crossed the street and was almost in the library door when Owen came back out. Owen held the door opwn and Shapiro nodded and went in the building, hoping he wouldn't lose Owen while he waited a decent interval before picking up the chase. When he went back outside, he couldn't see Owen but bounced across the entry apron to the sidewalk and checked both directions. There were more pedestrians than he remembered. His eyes had been glued to Owen and he had not paid much attention to anything else. His stomach sank, and he ran fifty yards or so in the direction from which they had approached the library before turning and running a much greater distance in the other. He was sweating and out of breath when he finally caught a glimpse of Owen's blond hair almost a full block ahead. He exhaled deeply and shook his head as he hurried to catch up. He was lucky. He had stupidly stayed too long in the library out of the crazy fear that Owen would be suspicious if they crossed paths again. No way Delaney would recognize him from that brief encounter. He was sure of that now; but even so, when Owen entered that little park and began his rounds there, Shapiro held so far back he often lost sight of Owen in the crowds.

He had no way of knowing what was said as Owen wandered along the park path, just as he had no way of knowing what was said at the library. But it seemed pretty obvious that Owen was asking about Doug Ranzone; and that he hadn't gotten any good answers yet. And it was just as obvious that Delaney didn't have any of those special skills at persuasion he himself had developed up in the City. In fact, Delaney looked a little intimidated by some of the homeless guys in the park. Maybe he should make his own rounds at some point. Delaney had apparently done enough homework to lead him to a specific patch of homelessness more than a thousand miles from his home base. If Delaney had done all the spadework, maybe he should just finish the job himself. What he should do is follow Delaney till he's done—at least for the day—and then retrace his steps and do a little digging himself.

Delaney's next stop was a three story wooden residential building in a sorry condition familiar to Shapiro from his slumlord days. Shapiro sat at a bench across the street from the building, at a bus stop, and called John

Rogers' answering service while Delaney spoke briefly to the two men smoking on the porch of the building and then went inside. Had he still been on the beat in New York, he'd have guessed the place was a crack house or maybe a copping area for opioid addicts. He snorted gently as he told himself it wasn't his problem; and waited for his call back. It came within minutes. Delaney was still inside the house.

"Okay. I've only got two minutes. What's happening?" Ranzone said.

"I'm still in Miami Beach, following Delaney on foot. He's making the rounds of homeless hangouts in the neighborhood around his motel. Obviously asking about your brother."

"And?"

"Don't look like he's had any luck yet, Guv. I'm waiting outside what I'd guess is a crack house. Delaney went in a few minutes ago."

"Geez. I was afraid of that. It was bad enough that Dougie was an acoholic."

"There's no tellin' that your brother's in there. It's just another stop on the trail, I think. But what do we do if he is. An addict, I mean?"

"Same plan. Grab him and get him out of there. We'll get him into rehab somewhere."

Shapiro spotted Delaney coming out of the house. "Hold on, Guv. Our blond reporter is leaving. Nobody with him. Good chance that means your brother wasn't inside."

"Or wasn't in shape to get dragged out." Ranzone sounded exhausted.

"Maybe. But Delaney's checking his map, like he's headed to another stop. That's probably good news. As far as your brother bein' an addict goes, I mean."

"Hope so. Let me know what happens as soon as you have something."

Ranzone finished his call to Shapiro with just enough time to scramble to the podium to give his speech to the VFW in Wilkes Barre. But he spoke through a fog. Though the crowd was sizeable, Shapiro's call and the whole Dougie mess had made it hard to concentrate on what he was doing. He felt half asleep, like he was addressing a distant, inattentive and faceless audience in an uncomfortable dream. But as he droned through the lines for his new "light pink" speech, two vague hopes, like faint background violin music, drifted into a kind of parallel consciousness. The first hope was that no one would find Dougie, that maybe he was dead. The second was that if

Delaney found him before Shapiro, no matter how far gone Dougie was, he would deny everything. Or maybe not even remember what happened in Philadelphia. In either event, Delaney's project would die.

But these two hopeful strains were subtly underplayed by a quiet *what if*. What if Dougie were still alive and neither Shapiro nor Delaney found him, leaving the gnawing, long-term worry that the story would eventually come out. Though, until recently, forcing that worry into his mind's recesses had become easier as each year passed without news from or about Doug, there would be no way he could repress the worry now. A suspicious Calderone or Shapiro might resort to blackmail. Or Delaney might take another approach to opening the Swenson case. His stomach twitched when what he'd begun thinking of as the Conry solution sounded a deep percussive note in the symphony.

The applause was tepid and he was shocked to realize he didn't care. It was only when Phil Conry spoke to him afterwards that he came back to life.

"You okay, boss? You were a little lifeless up there."

"You're right, Phil. I've been very tired. Any way we can cut back for a few days?"

"Doubt it, but I'll see. You still feel up to that hunting thing?"

The Pennsylvania Game Commission had declared a brief, special deer-hunting window for seniors during the week before the election and Ranzone had seen it as an opportunity to show off his gun creds and endear himself, so to speak, to the many Pennsylvanians for whom deer hunting was a sacred right. He had asked Phil to make a reservation for two days at a Pocono hunting lodge near Moosic and alert the press that the campaign would be suspended for those two days.

"Sure. It'll be a winner. And I'll enjoy it. Don't change those plans."

"Okay. If you say so. I'd bet you'll be the first gubernatorial candidate in the history of country to suspend his campaign to go hunting so close to the election. But it just might play." Conry opened his palms and shrugged. "Except of course for the animal rights crowd. But they'd never vote for a conservative *R* like Wright in any case." Before turning to leave, Conry said "My wife's got my time all planned. I'll miss the campaign but I'm sure I'll enjoy my time off as much as you will."

Ranzone felt lighter just thinking about tramping through the woods. But the lightness didn't last. Something about Phil's eagerness to serve actually pissed him off. He realized again that, if Phil hadn't needed to brag to Delaney about his hero John's thoroughness as an assistant DA, he'd never be in the mess he was in. He really liked Phil and always had. But he wished there was a way to make him less fatally transparent. After the election, if he kept Phil on, his being such a good guy could be a handicap for them both.

Chapter 29

The flophouse had been a complete bust. The longhaired manager was in a little office off the entry hall talking on the phone. Sounded like his girfriend. He cupped his phone in response to Owen's questions, and said he couldn't think of any Douglas or Doug or Dougie who'd been there in the three weeks he'd been at his job. When Owen asked if they had any records going back further, he waved Owen away and told him to get a police warrant if he wanted to proceed further and to close the door behind him. With that door closed and the manager's girlfriend conversation mooning on, Owen had wandered the halls of the makeshift hotel. A common bathroom off the second floor landing apparently served the entire building. All the other rooms of the house were divided into sleeping cubicles with flimsy wallboard partitions that did not go all the way to the ceiling. The few men—and they were all men—with whom he was able to speak seemed earnest enough. But none could place Doug. Most of the other men were either sleeping or nodding off in a drugged stupor. After a few minutes, Owen had done all he thought he could do and snuck past the manager's still closed door and left the building.

It was nearly six o'clock and the light outside was fading. Owen hoped it was a good hour to visit the Salvation Army, about ten blocks from the flophouse. By the time he walked there, the homeless might just be showing up for a meal and a bed for the night. He checked his map for the shortest route and began walking at a leisurely pace, a little relieved that the Salvation Army would be his last stop for the day. At his slower pace, he was enjoying the stroll. Like the rest of the neighborhood he had already walked through, most of the streets were lined with small, low-rise apartment buildings and larger stone residences that had been converted to apartments. But the streets were clean and canopied with attractive shade trees of a type unfamiliar to Owen, but more inviting than the rows of palm trees he would have expected.

The block on which the Salvation Army building was located was crowded with homeless. Both sexes, but again, more men than women. They were chatting in groups or stretched out on the shaded grass border between the sidewalk and the street, all apparently lined up to get in the building for the night. They were more approachable than the park or flop house people. More like the library crowd. In fact he thought he recognized the guy with the Larry Czonka Dolphin shirt and guessed that the library crowd and Salvation Crowd were the same, more put together than some other homeless in the area. He moved slowly down the walk, stopping to ask about Doug at each cluster of people. Some of them recognized Owen from the morning at the library; but no one could think of anyone in their community named Doug. It took about a half hour to move all the way along the line to the building entrance, which had not yet opened for business. A security guard sat on a metal folding chair by the door ready to funnel in the evening's guests when the time came. Owen asked him how he might get help finding a sixty-year old man who might stay there from time to time. He stretched the truth and told the guard that the man's family was searching for him. The guard held back the waiting line, unlocked the door to let Owen in the building and told him to go down the hall to Captain Mitchell's office.

In some ways the interior of the Salvation Army building reminded Owen of the prison where he had met Charles Swenson. It was not fancy, but it was extravagantly clean. He imagined some of the guests did a lot of cleaning in exchange for the goodies they received. The dark vinyl floor shone like the shoes of a West Point cadet. The spotless white walls were decorated with compulsively ordered portraits of uniformed Salvation Army administrators, with ranks from Lieutenant to Commissioner. Mitchell's office was at the end of the hall. His door was open.

Mitchell was in uniform, leaning back in his desk chair and reading when Owen knocked. He straightened and put down what he had been reading.

"Hello. Hello. Come in," he said. He had an earnest thirty-something face and a deeper voice that Owen expected from the boy-scout looks. "What can I do for you?"

Owen took the seat across from Mitchell before speaking. "I'm looking for someone, an older man, who might have stayed in your center. Not sure when it would have been but I know he was homeless and in this area two to four years ago."

"Well, if we did our job for him, he wouldn't still be around after four years. Not even two. This place is an emergency shelter. It's not permanent housing. Our job is to stabilize lives and get our people into their own housing. We do a lot of follow up, but sometimes we lose track of people. What your fellow's name?"

"Douglas Ranzone'" Owen spelled out Ranzone. And Mitchell swung around to his computer.

After a minute or so, Mitchell read from his screen. "No one by that name recently; but yes, we had a Douglas Ranzone here, looks like three years ago. We placed him as a dishwasher in a restaurant on South Beach and he apparently moved in with someone from work. We have the name of the restaurant. Nothing more than that."

"That would be a start if you could give it to me."

Mitchell turned back to his desk and wrote out the information on a small pad and tore off the top page. "Good luck," he said as he handed Owen the page. "Wish him well for us if you find him."

It was dark by the time Owen walked back to his motel; and he was hungry. The last food he'd had was on the plane from Philly. So he decided to kill two birds and drive to South Beach to eat at the restaurant where Doug had worked as a dishwasher. Maybe he still did work there. He went straight to his rental car in the lot, checked his map and found his way to South Beach within fifteen minutes. At a light at 14th and Washington Avenue, he called Barb. She was busy with the kids' nighttime routine so Owen hurriedly explained that he hadn't yet found his witness and would stay in Miami at least one night. Noticing his battery was low, he plugged the phone into the Honda's charger and set it on the passenger seat when the call was done.

The restaurant, called El Ranchero, was Argentinean, on Ocean Drive and 7th. Driving south on Ocean Drive at a snail's pace in a stream of high fashion cars whose drivers oogled the even higher fashion pedestrians they were inching by, Owen couldn't help but oogle as well. While there were some typical tourist types, the wide sidewalks were largely populated by the very beautiful. Exquisite young women and men dressed to show off their perfect bodies. Owen felt old and ordinary.

The restaurant itself was modestly upscale. Nothing glamorous. Owen checked his phone again and concluded it wasn't charged nearly enough to be useful, decided to leave it in the car while he ate, and slid it under the passenger seat to hide it from would-be thieves. He left his car with valet parking, crossed the umbrella studded patio and asked the hostess at the door for an inside table for one. If he was going to talk to someone about their kitchen help, inside would probably be better. It was not as crowded as the patio with its front row view of the Ocean Drive street scene; and it was quieter, without the clamor of hotshot drivers whistling or honking at the tightly clad young women parading alongside them.

The hostess sat Owen about halfway back in the house and, not long after a busboy served water, a waitress in black slacks and a gaucho blouse came by to introduce herself and take his order. Paulette was her name. Dark hair, pulled back. Pretty. She seemed genuinely friendly and Owen hoped she might be a good source of information. So he made up a lot of questions about the menu and when she answered them all without hesitation, he commented that she seemed well informed and asked how long she had worked at El Ranchero.

"About five years. I get all the hours I want and the tips are not bad."

"Good for you. Sounds like you've found the right spot. But what comes next?"

"No idea. I'm just twenty-seven so I don't worry about the future that much. I'll save my money and see what happens."

"Sounds like a plan." Owen turned back to his menu and said "I think I'll try the beef Milanesa, even though it doesn't sound very Argentinean. You said that's your favorite."

"Oh, it is. Argentinean. And my favorite. It was brought to Argentina ages ago by Italian imigrants. You'll like it. I guarantee."

Paulette gave Owen a choice of sides, suggested a glass of Argentinean Tempranillo (Owen nodded in agreement), entered Owen's order on a hand held computer device, and moved on to another table. Owen watched her work and noticed she spent time chatting with all her customers.

As Owen knew all good wait staff would do, Paulette came back to him when he had started his meal.

"Everything okay? Do you need anything?"

Owen put down his fork and held up one finger as he swallowed his bite of beef. "It's delicious. But I have a question for you."

Paulette eyed one of her other tables but smiled at Owen and said "Shoot."

"Since you've worked here so long, I thought you might know an old guy named Doug. Doug Ranzone. I was told he was dishwasher here."

Paulette didn't blink. "Sure, I knew Dougie. Nice guy, but a little off, I'd say. A lot of those dishwashers are. He died two Christmases ago. Hit by a car. But people say it was suicide. Walked right out on to the middle of the MacArthur Expressway. I heard he hung on for few days at Jackson

Memorial, but died anyway. I really didn't know him that well but it was sad to hear about it."

"Well, thank you. Sad to hear that news."

Owen finished his meal without engaging Paulette in additional conversation. In fact, he couldn't have chatted with her even if she'd sat at the table with him. Dougie dead? What did that mean for his case? His mind swirling with *what nows,* he felt exhausted and sagged in his seat. What he needed was fresh air or something to perk him up. He signaled Paueltte, mimed signing his check, and ordered a coffee when she arrived at his table. She added the coffee to her computerized order, printed out the check and asked the bus boy to bring Owen his coffee.

The coffee too was Argentinean, and strong. By the time he finished it, he felt a little less soggy. But he still needed some fresh air. He signed his bill, added a big tip for Paulette and left. Outside, he realized he didn't want to walk among the beautiful people. He knew he wasn't bad looking and his hair always brought attention, but he was no GQ or Vogue model like so many of the stars of the sidewalk. And he was wearing his tweed jacket and khakis, not exactly South Beach attire. So he crossed Ocean drive and walked through the park stretched between the sidewalk on that side and the beach. When he reached the beach, he inhaled deeply and continued past the sand volleyball courts on down almost to the water's edge. On the last stretch of dry sand he sat down and looked straight ahead. It was very dark, no moon and only a faint haze of light pollution from the activity on Ocean Drive, several hundred yards behind him. The waves beat amicably at the water line with a slow rhythm that settled him. He leaned forward and grabbed his knees, rocking gently, until he felt a violent yank from behind as someone put a stranglehold around his neck from the left side.

A deep voice with a New York accent said "Leave Doug Ranzone alone. Drop the story, or else."

Owen squirmed to turn toward his attacker, but the stranglehold just tightened and then he felt a sharp pain on the right side of his skull. And the rhythm of the waves slowed to a stop.

PART III
FROM THE ARMCHAIR INTO THE FIRE

Chapter 30

Shapiro had followed Delaney from the Salvation Army back to his motel. While he had no idea what had gone down at that Salvation Army, he told himself that, if Delaney had picked up anything good in there, he'd let it go till morning. At least, that's what he thought until Delaney went directly to his car and Shapiro could see him studying his map by the Honda's interior light. Shapiro grabbed the parking tickets from the windshield of his own car, thanking God it hadn't been towed from that hydrant, and started up his car as soon as Owen turned off the light. He followed Owen to South Beach where, by the time they hit the slow traffic of Ocean Drive, he was only four cars behind Delaney. Since two were open convertibles and one a low riding sports car, he had no trouble keeping an eye on Delaney's Honda and he couldn't help but notice the young crowd on the sidewalks. Beautiful girls. He told himself that even the best looking would end up in the Villages one day. But most of the elegant guys had that look he always took for gay, even if they had a beautiful lady draped all over them. He felt an instant dislike of the place.

When he saw Owen stopping at a restaurant he relaxed, again convinced that Owen was finished work for the day. He should've left Delaney to his meal and headed back to that park where those homeless toughs had given Delaney a hard time. He was sure he could force more co-operation than Delaney had. But he was hungry too. Nothing to eat since that Taco Bell. And, just maybe, Doug Ranzone worked at that restaurant. So he rolled up to the valet parking stand and followed Delaney into El Ranchero.

Shapiro was seated about thirty feet from Delaney and he watched Delaney closely. He saw nothing but a man ordering dinner alone, maybe a little friendly with his waitress. But that seemed innocent enough. As he himself enjoyed his Locro Stew, which his waiter had told him was like an Argentinean gumbo, but really wasn't, he tried to keep pace with Delaney whose meal had been served before his. When he saw Delaney ask for his check, he did the same and, after signing it, sat and waited for Delaney to finish his coffee. Reviewing his Miami day so far, his shoulders sagged a little as he realized all he had been doing is riding Delaney's coattails. He had done nothing but follow him around hoping he knew something. But he obviously didn't, except that Doug Ranzone was probably homeless somewhere in Bayshore. Well, now he knew that too. Shouldn't he get off his ass and do something for himself? He decided to follow Delaney when he left the restaurant and, once he was safely back inside that motel, strike out on his own. The image of a snapping alligator came to mind.

He searched his pockets for his valet ticket and quickstepped out of El Ranchero to the white shirted college kid at the valet stand, to get in line before Delaney. But when Delaney came outside, he walked across Ocean Drive and headed into the park that ran between the sidewalk on that side of the street and the beach further on. Shapiro breathed heavily as he waited for his car then, when it was brought to him, slipped in behind the wheel, rolled it further ahead in the valet zone and waited to see if Delaney was meeting anyone in the park. He soon lost sight of him and had to get out of the car and cross the street himself, yelling to the valet kids that he'd be right back. Once in the park, he could see Delaney walking toward the beach, then toward the water. He walked all the way to the knee-high wall that separated the park from the beach. From there had a good view for quite a distance. No one else on the beach. If Delaney was waiting for someone, his own showing up on the beach could cause alarm. So he held back. However, as Delaney got further away, the darkness hid him and Shapiro had to sneak forward. When he could again see Delaney clearly—he was now sitting not too far from the water's edge—he stopped again. Shifting his weight from leg to leg as he stood there doing nothing, Shapiro bit his lower lip and shook his head. Why wasn't he *doing* something? He'd bragged to Ranzone that he was good at persuasion. He should go persuade. He started toward Delaney.

When he got about sixty feet away, he could see that Delaney was rocking like he had a baby in his arms. Something about that faggy image pissed him off. Who the fuck was this guy? A writer for Madamoiselle? Hoping to become one of the big boys with this pathetic expose? He picked up a short heavy piece of driftwood that was lying nearby and snuck up behind Delaney. Fortunately, the middling sized waves were slapping the waters edge with enough of a splash that Delaney couldn't hear his soft steps on the packed sand. When he got close enough, he balanced the smooth driftwood in his right hand, swung his left arm around Delaney's neck and squeezed. In the most menacing voice he could muster, he told the wimpy looking writer to leave the Doug Ranzone story alone. When Delaney tried to break loose, Shapiro yanked again, but harder, and swung the driftwood at Delaney's head.

Chapter 31

When Owen awoke, he was in the dark. Literally and figuratively. There was no light whatsoever. The darkness was thick and oppressive, and his breathing faltered as it always did when claustrophobia began to overwhelm him. He sat up and hunted for his phone but it was not in his pocket. He pawed around the hard grainy floor on which he sat, but couldn't find it. Then he remembered he'd left it in his car, attached to a wire of some sort. The effort at remembering that little detail exhausted him and he eased himself down onto his back and closed his eyes again.

The next time he woke, he remembered he had no phone but also remembered he could get a little light from his fitbit. He pressed the "on" button. Still woozy, he couldn't read the blurry digits that would have told him the time; but he aimed the light from the fitbit around his cell, or whatever it was. The luminescence was too weak to help. He tried to stand but wobbled and sat down. Then, still fighting his claustrophobia, he lay back and closed his eyes again.

The third time he awoke was more productive. He could read his watch. It was four o'clock, AM he presumed, from the darkness. Though it could as easily be afternoon in a dark basement. He crawled around. The movement relieved some of his panic. He was not buried alive in an oversized coffin. He soon bumped into what felt like strips of plastic fabric connected to metal tubes. Like the floor, they too were gritty. Probably sand. He must still be near the beach. He fingered the metal tubes and concluded they were the frames of beach chairs. That would make sense of the plastic. He must be in some kind of storage shed for the beach chair concession. That would mean he was not in a dark cellar. That would mean it was four AM. He limped his way around the shed, feeling for a door, bumping as he went into what he now immediately recognized as beach umbrellas. He found what he thought was the door and pushed on it; but it was locked from the outside. It flexed some as he put his weight into it; but he did not have enough strength to force it open. He tried to remember if he'd noticed the shed on his walk to the water's edge. He couldn't remember, but guessed it had to be far enough back from the water to be safe in high tides. Maybe close enough to that park for someone to hear him.

Owen's croaked a few feeble calls for help. But he was weak, the effort was tiring, and he despaired of anyone hearing him. Probably wasn't anyone around at that hour anyway. He plunked himself down on his butt and stared at the hairline of faint light he could now detect outlining the shed door. He put his hand to the pounding ache on the right side of his head and felt what had to be dried blood. Then he laid himself down on his back and fell asleep again.

The loud conversation outside the shed woke Owen.

"What the fuck is this? Damn kids broke the lock. Closed it up with a fuckin' screw-driver. Hope they didn't trash our stuff."

A splash of light startled Owen as the door swung open. When he adjusted, he could see the shock on the faces of the two older men in sleeveless tee shirts who'd opened it. Then he saw the blood all over his clothes.

"What happened to you, man?"

"Don't know. Someone attacked me and threw me in here, I guess."

"They rob you?"

Owen patted his pockets, felt his wallet and said, "Don't think so."

The men glanced at Owen and gave each other wary glances. "Gay bashers," one said. The other said "Prob'ly. But looks like he needs help" and pulled a phone from his baggy shorts to made a call. Owen hung his head in relief.

Chapter 32

Shapiro had had a busy night. He realized he'd hit Delaney harder than he should've. His emotions got the best of him. Something about that rocking and that ridiculous hair—had to be dyed—screamed fairy and he swung too hard. He knew Delaney wouldn't wake up for a long while. He was pretty sure he hadn't killed Delaney—he'd hit lots of shitheads harder with his nightstick and they lived—but he thought it was best if he hid him away till daybreak. He looked around and saw a shed about a hundred yards down the beach, barely visible by the lights from Ocean Drive. Not a bad spot. He could improvise a lock and, if he couldn't himself get back early enough to quietly unlock it, someone else would be around in the morning for sure.

He dragged Delaney to the shed, saw it was already locked and ran back to his car for tools. It took only minutes to break the shed lock, haul Delaney inside and lock the door again with his screwdriver inserted in the hasp.

Then he drove to that homeless park. As he'd expected, the daytime crowd was still there, many of them bedding down for the night. He parked and walked along the gravel path like he had as a beat cop looking for troublemakers. He had long ago gotten this routine down pat: find the most hostile looking one and get into his face. A middle-aged guy with dramatic long, wavy, silver hair, leaning back on his bench, with arms crossed and legs spread in front of him, followed Shapiro with half-closed eyes, like a lizard. Shapiro walked up to him and asked "You know a guy named Doug Ranzone?"

The lizard didn't answer. Shapiro kicked one outstretched leg. "I said, 'you know a guy named Doug Ranzone'." The lizard stood up. He was maybe two inches taller than Shapiro. Perfect. He leaned into Shapiro and said "We told your partner—or was the blond your boyfriend—we don't know no Doug. So leave us alone."

Shapiro turned as though to leave; but violently swung his body back, elbow leading the turn, and hammered it into the lizard's gut. As the lizard bent forward, Shapiro grabbed his right hand, which was knotted into a fist, and twisted the entire arm behind the lizard's back. "Sir, I asked you nicely if you know Doug Ranzone." Shapiro knew the old punk didn't want to lose face. But neither did he. So he bent the lizard's arm with more force until he heard a bone crack and the lizard cry out "Fuck, you broke my arm"!

Shapiro released the broken arm and panned a sneer at the crowd that had gathered. He pulled back the flap of his jacket to expose his shoulder holster. "Any a you know a Doug. . . . or Dougie . . . or Douglas?"

A sheepish teenaged boy, skinny, maybe strung out, asked "What's he look like?"

"You tell me," Shapiro said.

"There's a kid comes in here on a bike every once in a while. I think his name's Doug."

Progress. But obviously not Ranzone's Doug. He looked around again. "Anyone else?"

By now the entire congregation was within ten feet of Shapiro and the groaning lizard, whispering to each other. Within a few minutes, he had four more Doug suggestions, none beyond middle age. He was frustrated but satisfied they knew nothing.

He pointed his chin toward the lizard, now slumped on his bench and using his good arm to press the broken one to his side, and said "He'll live, but you oughta take your friend here to the hospital."

It was about one o'clock when he arrived back at El Ranchero after a more civilized but equally useless conversation with the few homeless still hanging out at the library. The valet parking was closing and he pulled into the "no parking" zone. There were still too many people around to risk freeing Delaney, so he sat. By the time the valet drivers lugged their stand back into the restaurant and left, his eyes were drooping. Giving in after a half-hour or so, he closed them and slept fitfully until the sun came up, then got out of his car and crossed Ocean Drive to the park and across the sand to within fifty feet of the shed. No one around yet. He could see the screwdriver still holding the door shut; but he couldn't hear Delaney. That might be a problem. He should be hearing all sorts of screaming by now.

On the off chance that Delaney was dead, he opted for a wait and see, moving back to the park wall and taking a seat with a good view of the shed. At about eight, two older guys in sleeveless tee shirts approached the shed and opened the door. One of them made a phone call. Within minutes, an ambulance wailed up Ocean Drive and pulled into the park, stopped, and let out two medics carrying a furled stretcher.

When the ambulance left with its new patient inside, Shapiro followed it to the emergency entrance to Jackson Memorial Hospital.

Chapter 33

Owen was conscious on the ride to the hospital. The bleeping wails from the ambulance siren kept him awake. But his mind was sluggish and it was hard to make sense of the scattered thoughts that rolled around his tired brain. For one, why was he mugged? Those guys from the chair concession had guessed he was attacked because he looked gay. His lean build and silky hair did occasionally give people that impression. But struggling to come up with something better, he could only guess that it was someone from that homeless park who knew Doug. But why attack him if Doug was dead? Could Paulette have been wrong? Was she thinking of someone else? Or was she too trying to protect Doug with that suicide story? If so, could his attacker have been Dougie himself?

By the time they reached the hospital and the medics wheeled him into emergency, he had a vague plan. First, make sure that Dougie was dead. Now that he knew the approximate date of death and the hospital where Dougie had supposedly died, he could check on the Internet to confirm it. But whether Dougie was or wasn't dead, the mugger's comment about forgetting that story still puzzled him. What story? Did they take him for a news reporter? What could those homeless guys think was so interesting about Doug that he'd warrant a news article. Could they possibly know—or suspect something—about Doug? So, once he was released, despite some trepidation about it, he'd have to go back to that park.

The stay in the emergency room took hours, from the initial treatment of his wound, which required a couple of stitches and a shaving of a patch of his hair, through the completion of a concussion protocol and other tests. It was two in the afternoon before he saw the light of day and called up an Uber ride from the hospital to El Ranchero. He had been told not to drive for two days, but he was worried about the rental car remaining too long in valet parking. Fortunately the restaurant was open. He fished his ticket from his sport coat pocket and handed it to the same kid to whom he'd turned the car over the previous night. When the kid stared at the blood on Owen's clothes, Owen said, "Had an accident. Spent the night in the hospital."

"Lucky we didn't have it towed," the kid said and ran off to fetch the Honda.

When he pulled the car to the curb, Owen staggered into it and drove slowly back to Bayshore where his first stop was his motel. He showered and changed clothes. Checking his wound in the mirror, he was relieved to see so little hair shaved off his head. With some artful combing, he was able to fully obscure the bandage.

At the library, he got a few nods from the women on the benches outside as he headed directly to the door. Inside he asked for a public computer and was directed to a glass walled room to the left. Once in the room, he had to sit on a stiff library chair and wait for a computer to come free. A sign said "No More Than Thirty Minutes Per Session," so he didn't expect too long a wait. Nevertheless, after thirty minutes, the machines were all still occupied. So he stood impatiently behind an old guy with ZZ Top beard until the man turned, frowned, and got up.

Sitting on the warm seat, Owen called up the Florida Death Certificate archive and plugged in the name of Douglas Ranzone, with a possible death at Jackson Memorial Hospital on December 26th, two years before. No information. He tried December 27th. Again nothing. He hit paydirt with December 28. Doug had indeed died in the very same hospital Owen himself had been treated that morning. No next of kin named. Suspicious about that possible suicide Paulette had alluded to, and what might have driven Dougie to such a step, he called up the Miami Herald for front-page news in the days before that Christmas. This time, it took going *backwards* three days before he found an article about an older woman strangled to death in the Bayshore area of Miami Beach.

Okay, so Doug was indeed dead. That last strangling ramped up his guilt, which finally got the best of him and his death was more likely a suicide than an accident. So why would someone mug him for making inquiries about a dead man? He couldn't answer that question. But maybe someone at the park would. Or maybe someone at that park had been an accomplice in that strangling and was afraid Owen was on his scent. He left his car on the street at the library and, finally heeding the emergency room advice, walked to the park.

The park was again crowded; and a number of heads followed him with interest as he walked the gravel path. Interest, he thought, not suspicion or aggression like the previous day. But he did notice one big, longhaired guy with a cast on his arm coolly walk out the side exit. Owen stared. He remembered the hair from the previous day, but not the cast. Ruling out the possibility that, with the broken arm, he was the guilty friend of Dougie's who attacked him, he asked some of the more curious others what happened to the big guy's arm. It was not long before he learned the story of a fight that had gone down in the wee hours the previous night.

One skinny young kid in jeans and tee shirt said "He was looking for that Doug guy too. And he had a gun."

Owen took the only empty bench space he could find and sat motionless for a few seconds. Then he waived the skinny kid toward his bench where a brief conversation filled in the blanks a bit. The big fight had occurred about twelve thirty or one, a short while after his own mugging. The guy with the gun was about Owen's height, six feet, about fifty years old, medium build, with a strong New Yawk accent. By the time he dragged himself out of the park, Owen was convinced that his attacker and the New Yawk inquisitor were one and the same. So what did that mean?

Only Shultz and Barb knew he had gone to Miami, and neither of them knew where in Miami he'd ended up. And neither of them would have answered any stranger's probing questions without calling him first. Was it possible that the Reverend Garcia alerted someone? Told them where Owen would be searching for Dougie? Maybe Dougie had confessed his crimes to Garcia and Garcia felt protective of Doug.

By the time he meandered back to his car at the library, Owen had discarded the Reverend Garcia hypothesis. Well, maybe not discarded it; but concluded that it was unlikely. If Garcia had been close enough to Dougie to be worried for him, he would probably know that Dougie was dead. And, unless Garcia feared he would somehow be accused of harboring a serial strangler, or something like that, it made no sense that he would try to scare Owen off. He could have easily been uncooperative in the first place. And Owen had implied to Garcia that he was representing Dougie's family. He'd never said anything about writing a story. So unless all the unlikelies about Garcia were more likely than Owen thought, and Garcia just assumed he was a reporter interested in tracking down Doug, none of the Garcia business jibed with his attacker's warning about the "story".

Owen found himself fighting the conclusion that he had been followed all the way from Philadelphia, as unbelievable as that theory seemed when it first occurred to him. How that happened, he couldn't even guess. His trip was an impulse. He decided to go only the night before his flight. He sat in his car across from the library and breathed deep, serious breaths until he decided that, since Doug was dead, none of it made any difference. There was nothing more he could do in Florida.

Chapter 34

Shapiro had had enough experience with head smashing and emergency rooms to know that Owen would probably not be admitted to the hospital, that he'd be discharged directly from the emergency room. So he waited in a parking spot about thirty yards from the emergency room door. It took longer than he expected and his stomach was growling. When Delaney finally came out, he stopped just outside the door and made a phone call, then leaned against the hospital wall checking the phone every minute or so. He'd probably called Uber.

When the black sedan that picked Owen up left the hospital lot, Shapiro followed. The sedan dropped Owen off at the restaurant where he picked up his rental car. But then he drove to the library, went in and stayed a long time. Shapiro waited a frustrating half hour, then marched across the street to find out what Delaney was doing. After a frantic search, he saw him glued to a monitor in a glass walled computer room. He chose not to go in, but waited at an empty table faking interest in a magazine grabbed from nearby rack until, after a few minutes, Owen came out of the room and left the library.

Following Delaney on foot to the homeless park, Shapiro found himself hoping that all Delaney had been doing at that computer was checking flight schedules for a trip back to Philadelphia. All this futile tracking of Delaney tracking Dougie was irritating, and he wanted to call this part of the gig quits. When Delaney spent only a few minutes in the homeless park before strolling back to his car at the library, Shapiro was more convinced than just hopeful that Delaney was heading home. He called the John Rogers answering service.

At his motel, Owen phoned American Airlines and made a reservation for the first flight to Philly that he could catch without a frantic rush. He checked out of the motel and drove carefully to the airport where he returned his Honda to Budget, inched through security, and found himself at his gate with forty-five minutes to spare. Tired, with an aching head and sore back, he wriggled into one of the immovable leather chairs lined up to face the check-in podium, hoping to doze for a half hour or so. But he couldn't get comfortable and decided to put off sleep till the plane ride itself, while he forced himself to focus on the Dougie mystery.

If he had been followed from Philadelphia, that would suggest that either Conry or Ranzone was having him tailed even while he was there. But why would they do that? He couldn't believe that Glassman would have reported his Apache Tear theory to Ranzone. And it was unlikely that Father Bill was suspicious of him. He had been too helpful for that. But maybe Ranzone had learned from Father Bill that Owen wanted to talk to Dougie and Ranzone assumed he'd be going to Florida. Or maybe Zapo had called him. However it happened, the fact that he had been followed, and threatened on top of that, meant that Ranzone wanted his search stopped, probably because he had done exactly what Owen suspected. It also had to mean that Ranzone didn't know Dougie was dead.

It was eleven thirty, about the time Shultz had his hour break between classes. Owen called and, when he heard Geoff's booming voice, felt like a child finding his misplaced father in a huge Home Depot or sports stadium. The perky red-head sitting next to him, however, turned in surprise when she heard the blast. Owen moved away.

"Geoff? Owen."

"Yes buddy. Where are you? What's up?"

"I'm at the airport in Miami. Coming home. But I've learned that Dougie is dead—" Owen paused, and Shultz interrupted.

"Well that makes things easier. Or harder, not sure which."

"Harder. I think. Or at least a little more scary. I was mugged and threatened down here. Even had to go to the hospital. Whoever did it seemed to think Dougie was still alive."

"What happened?"

"Some strong arm told me to forget about the Doug Ranzone story and then hit me on the head. With a club or something."

"What story?"

"Beats me. Sounds like he thought I was a reporter."

"That doesn't make sense."

"I agree. But that's what he said. Maybe someone in Ranzone's campaign hired him, told him that I was digging up dirt for his opponent and had to be stopped."

"That could be. If it was Ranzone behind this, he sure as hell wouldn't tell the guy the truth."

"Right. And if it was Ranzone—and who else could it be?—doesn't that confirm he did what I think he did?"

"Probably—at least as planting that black stone goes. But it doesn't really say anything about his brother's guilt. He's probably still just guessing at that." Owen could hear Shultz breathing while they both waited in silence. Finally, Shultz asked "How'd you learn the brother was dead?"

"A waitress at the restaurant where he worked a couple years ago told me. And I confirmed it on the state death certificate website."

"Hmm. If you could find it, why not Ranzone, or his guy down there?"

"You need to know the date of death and maybe the hospital to look it up. The waitress gave me that. I was mugged shortly after we talked, so I have to guess Ranzone's guy had no clue what she told me."

"Right. Unless he heard your conversation with the waitress or went back to her and found out after he mugged you."

"I suppose they're both possible. But he was still haranguing some of the homeless in the area, looking for Doug well after I was out cold."

"So he has no idea what you found out. Or didn't."

"Right."

Shultz went silent again for a while, then said "Actually, if Ranzone's guilty, and he doesn't know his brother's dead, he may think you've got something on him, now that you're coming back to Philadelphia."

"Unless he thinks the threat scared me into leaving."

"That would be best for you. But unless his man learns the brother's dead, he'd never be sure what happened down there. You could be in some danger. Maybe he'd think a threat was not enough to shut you up."

Owen said nothing but could hear Barb groaning "not again, Owen." In fact, he was thinking the same thing. Eventually, he asked "If you were Ranzone, what would you do? Have me killed?"

"Such things have been known to happen. Yes."

"Ug." Owen's shoulders dropped two inches. "But he just doesn't seem the murdering type."

"What type is that? I just read an article in the Times about an English lawyer who defended only murderers. Said anyone could commit a murder; and a good person who had done something bad was a better client than a truly bad person. He also said they were happy people, having gotten rid of a big problem in their lives." Shultz paused as though he wished he hadn't said what he'd said; but continued "If you were afraid your entire career was goin' down the drain for something you did before it ever really started, wouldn't you be desperate? Maybe his buddy Conry would take it on himself to fix the problem."

"Okay but let's think about this some more. No matter how he got my name, he has to associate me with the Innocence Project. I told Conry. And Father Bill. I didn't mention it to his friend Zapo, but if Ranzone talked to Zapo, he had to put two and two together. If he . . ." Owen couldn't bring himself to say the word on the tip of his tongue . . . "put me out of commission, he might assume, correctly I hope, that the people at the Innocence Project would be suspicious."

"Okay. So he's knows who you are and knows what you're up to. But also knows that, as you say, putting you out of commission could backfire on him. So what does he do? Hope you give up? No. For all he knows you've found his brother and will be ready to spring him when they re-open Swenson's trial, or whatever."

Owen tried to envision the scenario that Ranzone could be playing in his head. Innocence Project appeals Swenson's case on the basis of the Phillies ticket and maybe some kind of confirmation of Swenson's debt to Phelan. At the new trial, they cross examine Greg Stuart and create reasonable doubt about his testimony. And then they bring on Dougie, or maybe Alice or Father Bill, and confirm that collection of Apache Tears. Next would be Conry, who confirms that Ranzone himself had found the Apache Tear at the crime scene days after the stabbing.

Owen had to agree with Shultz. Unless Owen had fantasized the whole story, Ranzone would have to do something. And only Conry and he, himself, could conceivably tell the pieces of what appeared to be a Dougie coverup story. Holding out a feeble hope that his association with the Innocence Project would protect him, Owen felt chills when he considered Phil Conry's exposure. There was no way he was part of the cover-up. He'd been the one to brag about Ranzone finding that Apache Tear. After a silence prolonged enough for the entire courtroom drama to unfold again in his mind, he summarized it for Shultz.

Shultz went silent for a bit when Owen finished his thesis, then asked "You think you should warn Conry? Tell him the story? Tell him you were threatened down there?"

Owen's mouth opened and he breathed more heavily. "Maybe I should. Talk to him. He's probably in the dark about the whole thing. And if I told him about the stranglings down here that followed Doug wherever he went, he might at least be wary."

"And if he doesn't believe you and tells Ranzone?"

"That wouldn't change things much. Either I'm a kook or we both stay vulnerable to a murderous cover-up."

"Risky. But I guess you're right. Give him a call."

Chapter 35

The answering service called while Ranzone was lunching with two state reps from Montgomery County at a dark restaurant in Norristown that was trying its best to be elegant. They'd heard about Ranzone's planned hunting trip and wanted to go with him. Thought it would be good politics for them too and, hopefully, deductible as a campaign expense. Ranzone refused. He told them he had lined up some good old boys from the hunting lodge to go out with him. Not true. He hadn't made arrangements with anyone. But he didn't like the idea of hunting with pols. Too easily interpreted as the stunt it was. He could always go out alone, or find a partner when he got there. And besides, he was supposed to leave that night.

He had excused himself from the lunch table when the answering service called, gone outside to DeKalb Street, and moved away from the smokers huddled by the door to call Shapiro. He hadn't spoken to him since the previous afternoon while Shapiro staked out that drug house, and he had been wildly ruminating since then.

"Okay, where do we stand?" he said when Shapiro answered his call.

"Your boy Delaney is heading home. Empty handed. He didn't find your brother and a little persuasion last night looks like it convinced him to quit."

"That's good."

"Yeah, but the bad news is I didn't find him either. What do you want me to do?"

Elated that Delaney had failed, Ranzone sucked in a long, hard breath, threw his shoulders back and exhaled forcefully before saying "Try one more day and then forget about it if you don't find him. He may be dead for all we know. Or gone from Miami. Who knows? As long as Delaney didn't find him."

"That I'm sure of, Guv."

"Great news" Ranzone took another very deep breath. "One more day and then call me with your bill." He was about to end the call when his chest seized and his breathing stopped. Suppose, Dougie or no Dougie, Delaney refused to give up and tried some other way to prove Dougie was the Strangler. If he did, Conry was his best bet and Delaney would try to meet him and set out his case. No phone call would work for what Delaney needed to do; so someone should be watching Delaney twenty-four seven, at least until the election.

He told Shapiro to give him a second to think, then said "Listen. Maybe you should get your Philadelphia friends to tail Delaney up here until the election. Just in case. Maybe he's got something else planned."

"Fine with me. It'll be tight picking him up at the airport. But I think I know how they should do that. Fortunately, they know what he looks like. And where he lives, if they miss him there. I'll get right on it."

"Thanks. But keep me informed every step of the way."

"Will do, Guv." Shapiro paused, then said "by the way Gov, I was wondering if you knew of any good investment opportunities in your state. Anywhere, anything. But real estate is what I know best. I like to buy properties that are in the path of progress. Any paths you know of that might interest me? I think I done a good job down here and I'd never tell anyone about your brother, even if I find 'em."

"Not offhand." Ranzone could feel his blood race at the veiled blackmail. "But if something comes up, I'll let you know."

"Thanks, Guv."

Phil Conry was driving that day and, after lunch, they headed to East Falls where Ranzone had to pack his hunting gear before having his regular driver take him to the Poconos. Phil was energized by the prospect of his own break from the campaign. He rambled on about it and Ranzone felt that same nagging anger at Phil. He was such a puppy dog. Relentlessly positive and eager. Had he not been so cooperative and given that detail about the Apache Tear to Delaney, Delaney would never have even thought of looking for Dougie. Yeah, it was good that Delaney hadn't found Dougie; but suppose, like he said to Shapiro, Delaney kept pushing. Somehow. Suppose he convinced the Innocence Project to appeal the Swenson case without Dougie on the stand. Maybe that Phillies ticket. Maybe the too-pat testimony by Phelan. And they never found any blood on that knife, or anywhere in Swenson's flophouse. What does that do to Greg Stuart's testimony? Suppose an appeals court thought that was enough to retry the case. Would a judge permit Phil's testimony about the Apache Tear even though it had never been mentioned at the trial twenty years ago?

Ranzone slumped in his seat and gazed out his window to shake thoughts of those horrid possibilities. But they wouldn't shake away. And to make matters worse, he dreaded an endless ordeal of Shapiro sucking him for a payback that he would probably have to make if the possibility of a disclosure remained out there. He wanted sleep, anything to get away. He looked sideways at Phil, who was whistling faintly, and he had to hold back a groan. He felt faint, but when he imagined himself giving a solemn eulogy for Phil, his pulse quickened. He sat up and breathed deeply to cleanse the image from his mind and told himself there had to be another way. But the elegance of the solution kept forcing itself on him.

A sudden recollection of the almost comical story about Dick Cheney shooting a hunting partner made an accident with Phil seem a realistic possibility. He could picture it. The whole thing. Inexperienced hunter moving to the wrong place; maybe not wearing the right vest. Mistaken for a deer. He imagined the relief he'd feel. He could make sure Phil's family was provided for, of course. When he was elected, he could even have a building named after him. Or something like that. Of course, he might lose some votes from hunters who thought he was drunk or an asshole for shooting his hunting partner. So he'd have to make sure it was a perfect accident, not just carelessness or stupidity. Oh God! To banish the image of a bloody Phil, inert on a bed of fallen leaves in the woods, he squeezed his eyes shut with such force that they hurt. He shouldn't be thinking these things. Was he losing his mind?

They drove on in silence. As they crossed the Philadelphia city line, Ranzone turned to face Phil. He was still puckered up for that stupid whistling, as he tapped an upbeat rhythm on his steering wheel. Ranzone wanted to smack him.

"Hey Phil. Why don't you come hunting with me?"

Phil's whistling stopped and his lip dropped. Eyes bugging, he turned to face Ranzone. "You know I don't hunt, John."

"But I think you could use the relaxation."

"I'm plenty relaxed, John. And besides, my wife has the time all laid out for me. Movie tonight, Elton John concert at the Spectrum tomorrow night. And she wants us all to go to church on Sunday. Thinks it would be good for the kids if we all went together."

The thought of ending Phil's family bliss was no more that a pinprick to Ranzone's heart now that he saw that his own worries could be wiped away with one timely shot. Of course, afterward, he'd have the guilt to deal with. But he'd gotten used to living with that over the years. And what was worse? More guilt? Or humiliation and a prison sentence? He could feel his heart tighten up.

"I'm sorry, Phil. But the more I think about it, the more I think I'll need you around the lodge. No matter how hard we've tried to discourage them, the press will be all over the place. I'm gonna need your help."

"Oh boy. Roz is gonna be pissed. She's been planning this weekend since you came up with the idea."

"So sorry about that. But at least you'll get some enjoyment out of it. There's nothing more relaxing than being out in the woods, connecting to the natural world. I've loved it since the very first time I tried."

"Yea, I'm sure it could be fun. But I've never done it. And I don't even have a rifle. Can't hunt with a pistol, I assume. Would I actually have to go out stalking a deer?"

"I think it would be best if you went out with me. The special season is for seniors only and you're not a senior yet, but I don't think that'll be a problem. And I've got plenty of rifles. Your being in the woods'll reduce the appearance of a political stunt. Your work would start when we got back and were shocked to see press at the lodge. You'd have to deal with them."

Conry drove on for a while in silence, then said "I guess Roz can find someone else for the concert tomorrow night. And the movie will be playing for a while. But believe it or not, I'll miss going to church with the kids the most." He sighed and said "Roz'll be very happy when this campaign is over."

"Me too," said Ranzone. "Only five more days." Ranzone blew a long breath through his own puckered lips. "Of course, when we win, we won't have much rest either. Lots of work to do putting together an administration." He leaned forward and turned toward Conry so Conry could see his face while driving. "You're gonna be a big part of that, Phil."

"I know," said Phil. "I'm looking forward to it."

The pinprick in Ranzone's heart went a little deeper when he calculated how much Phil and his family depended on him. But he saw no other way. To govern with the threat of exposure hanging over him would be agonizing, almost impossible. No question, Phil was the most elegant solution. And the opportunity was at hand.

Chapter 36

Owen could not get past voice mail on Conry's cell phone. Before his flight took off, he left two messages telling Conry it was urgent that he call back as soon as possible. And when the flight arrived in Philadelphia, he called again from the tarmac before disembarking and two more times at stops along the concourse to the airport exit. The last call was answered by a woman.

"Hello, Phil Conry's phone."

"May I speak to Mr. Conry?"

"He's not here. This is his wife. May I help you?"

Owen's heart sank. It would be one thing to tell Conry himself that he might be in danger; but, if Barb was a measure, even suggesting the danger to Phil Conry's wife would be a big mstake.

"Do you know how I can reach him? It's important."

"About the campaign?"

"Yes." Owen said to himself that that was at least partially true.

"Well he's with John. On that stupid hunting trip. He forgot his phone."

"Hunting trip? Stupid?"

"Oh, sorry. I shouldn't have said that. It's just that John made Phil go with him at the last minute. Phil has never been hunting in his life. Doesn't even have a rifle. But John was insistent. And Phil and I had plans." Mrs. Conry hesitated before saying "Phil didn't think he could refuse. John has been under a lot of strain the last couple of weeks and hasn't been feeling well. But I suppose if you're with the campaign, you noticed it too."

Owen didn't respond to the question, thinking he himself may have been the cause of some of that strain. He said "Do you know where they went? I don't have it with me."

"Yes, he wrote it down somewhere. Should I get it?"

"If you would, please. I really have to reach him."

Owen could hear Mrs. Conry's footfalls as she walked around the house with the phone looking for the information. Finally, she came back on and said "Found it. They're at the Mountain Top lodge near Old Forge. It's in the Poconos. You want the number? And address?"

"Yes, please."

Owen tapped the information into his contacts, thanked Mrs. Conry and jogged down the concourse toward the connection for the SEPTA line out of the airport.

As he waited for the train to Suburban Station where he could get a local back to Chestnut Hill, he began to worry about Barbara. If he told her all that had gone down, she'd tell him to call the police, or at least Kopinski. But that would be a futile exercise. If he didn't tell her, he'd have to make up some explanation for the bandage on his skull. All he really wanted to do was tell Conry to be wary. While Ranzone's sudden demand that Conry go hunting was suspicious, given what he believed about Ranzone, his suspicion would be laughable to the police, even to Kopinski. No, he was better off not seeing Barbara until he had spoken to Conry. So he changed course and headed for the car rental counter.

Standing in line, he called Barb and told her he was back in Philadelphia and all was well. But he had to drive up to the Poconos to talk to one more person involved in the Swenson case. He expected to be home the next day. Saturday at the latest.

"Okay, Owen. But the kids keep asking when you're coming home. I think I'll tell them Saturday, just to be sure."

"Good idea." The Avis desk clerk signaled Owen forward and he said to Barbara "Listen, I've got to go. I'm at the car rental place." He felt a little woozy from all the half-truths he'd been telling Barbara. It was not like him. "See you soon. Miss you. Love you." He hoped this was the end of the subterfuge.

The Avis map was all he needed to start. He knew his way to the Poconos, up Interstate 476, and the map suggested the best exit for Old Forge would be Moosic. He'd ask directions or use the GPS from there. He hated using the GPS for routes he knew himself. That relentlessly pleasant voice telling him what to do.

It was still bright for late afternoon, with two days left of daylight savings. The traffic on the Interstate was moderate. Hunters taking advantage of the special deer shoot, weekenders taking advantage of what would probably be one of the last good weekends before winter. It took four hours, with a break at the Route 80 interchange, to reach the Moosic exit. Darkness had already fallen.

At the end of the off ramp he stopped and plugged the lodge address into the GPS. A message appeared telling him that some of the route was on unmarked roads. He'd probably have to ask directions when he got closer. The lodge must be on an old timber road. He hoped there were people around to ask. Maybe there would be a sign.

The bullet holed sign on Lonesome Road said the population of Old Forge was eight thousand some. But the parts he passed on the route to the lodge were almost deserted. Lonesome Road had a white clapboard church not far from the town limit and, down the road a mile or so, a short commercial strip with at least one in three of its shops shuttered. It was after eight and only a Dollar Store and a gas station/convenience store were open. He stopped at the gas station. His tank was half full; but he slipped his credit into the pump and, while his tank was filling, went inside for directions and a Coke.

An obese country type, flannel shirt and overalls, sixtyish but maybe as young as forty five—hard to tell—eyed Owen as he plucked his can of coke from the cold drink cabinet. He asked for a dollar when Owen set the Coke on the counter in front of him. It took a great effort for him to speak or move. Owen wanted to be disgusted with the guy for letting himself go to the point where tasks of everyday life were such a struggle, but then wondered if he should feel sorry for him. Maybe he had some heart or lung disease. Owen gave him a five and asked if there was a good place to eat nearby.

"Nope. Your best bet is what we got here. Unless you wanna drive allaway back to the Interstate. Everything's shut up for the night. . . . or for good." He coughed when he tried to laugh at his own joke.

Owen tweezed two hot dogs rotating in an infra-red hot box, inserted them into two semi-stale rolls and slathered some mustard on both. He put them in oblong hot dog trays, and brought them to the counter. The ol' counterman didn't offer him a bag or a napkin. Three dollars. After stuffing his change into his pocked, Owen asked about the Mountain Top Lodge.

"Yeah, I know it. It's where the hot shits go to hunt." He coughed again. "From what I hear it's great hunting, but they don't let just anybody in. You a hunter?" He curled his lower lip as he asked.

"No. Just looking for someone. He's supposed to be hunting this weekend."

"The old guy reached under his counter and pulled out a brown bag which he set down in front of him like an exam paper. He then took the ballpoint pen from the coffee cup next to the credit card machine and began to draw. Breathing hard through his nose, it took him several minutes to produce a rough but intelligible map, with landmarks and turns Owen would need to find the Lodge."

When he spun it around for Owen to see, Owen asked, "is this to scale?"

"Whadya mean?"

Owen felt foolish, after the guy had labored so for him. "What I mean is how long should it take me to get there. Or say to this turn." He pointed to the first turn off the main road they were on.

"Whole thing, forty five minutes. That turn there's about fifteen minutes."

Owen thanked the guy, bought two Snickers bars and left. It was very dark and quiet when he went outside.

Chapter 37

Phil Conry dropped John off at the lodge with his guns and both of their suitcases and rolled their car to the parking area about one hundred woodsy yards away. Though the place was not well lit, he could see that this was no rustic hunting lodge. Walking back from the lot, he passed a giant satellite dish and, when he approached the lodge, could hear a TV blasting the play by play of a football game into the still air. Inside, sure enough, a crowd of older Orvis-clad men sat around the largest and loudest TV he'd ever seen, drinking. Some beer, but mostly hard stuff. John was not there, but a fit younger man, maybe fortyish, with a military bearing, in jeans, turtleneck and a multi-pocketed vest, got up and escorted Phil to a room.

"Your things are in here. Mr Ranzone is in that room," he said, pointing down the hall.

Phil made a quick inspection of his room. Knotty pine walls, window to the woods that might give a nice view in the morning when he could actually see out, floors of large terra cotta tile with most of their open area splashed with rag-woven rugs, double bed and separate bathroom with shower. Nice. He went down the hall and knocked on John's door.

When John opened the door in shorts and an undershirt, he looked ashen. He had not spoken very much on the drive from Philadelphia; and Phil was worried he might be ill. John had been practically catatonic since the Route 80 exit on the Interstate when he got a brief call on one of his cell phones and then called someone named Curt. Phil didn't recognize the name. No one named Curt was associated with the campaign; and John's cryptic conversation hadn't given any clue as to what the call was about. The only words Conry and John had exchanged since that call were when John asked to stop at the gas station in Old Forge where he said he had to use the head, and then at the Dollar Store down the road a bit where he hoped he could buy some ammo.

Seeing how wrung out John looked as he swayed in the doorway, Phil didn't want to disturb him; but thought a little good news might help.

"John, I took a long look at the guys around that TV. No familiar faces from the press. So, unless they're in bed or still on their way, the press may not be coming. That should make the weekend easier for you."

"Thanks Phil. I'd invite you in, but I'm feeling very tired. Early start tomorrow. Everybody will be up and about at six thirty."

"Okay. I'll leave you be, John. See you in the morning."

Ranzone closed the door on Conry and shuffled to his bathroom where he stared at his reflection in the mirror but could focus only on the fear in his own eyes. He had worked all afternoon to steel himself for the shot at Phil he knew he had to take, but the call from Shapiro telling him that Delaney was also headed north on 476 frightened him. The news was like a stab in the heart and he'd told Shapiro to call his tail off. Though he had no idea how Delaney had learned where he and Phil were headed, his whole body had frozen with the certainty that Delaney'd turn up at the lodge. Now, alone in his bathroom, breathing became difficult and even the modest effort it took to brush his teeth and wash up had taxed him. Maybe he should get a check up when the campaign was over. He felt like the fat guy at the gas station whom he'd tipped ten bucks to call him if anyone stopped by asking for directions to Mountain Top Lodge. The guy had wheezed and coughed, barely able to acknowledge what he'd been asked to do. The woman in the Dollar Store seemed a little healthier, but he wasn't quite sure she understood her assignment either.

It was easier to breathe once he stretched out on his bed and propped two pillows under his head. When his phone rang, he struggled to sit up. He didn't recognize the number; but from the area code, guessed it was the guy from the gas station or the woman from the Dollar Store. He answered.

"Sir, this is Clem from the Stop and Fill on Lonesome Road." The caller coughed and took a labored breath. "You wanted to know if anyone was looking for the lodge." Another labored breath. "Well one just left. I gave him directions. Suppose that was okay. He'd find it one way or another."

While Clem was catching his breath, Ranzone asked "What'd he look like?"

It took a few seconds before Clem was able to answer. "Ordinary lookin'. But had very blond hair."

Ranzone thanked Clem for the information and lay himself back down. His own breath was again labored, even lying flat on his back. He stared at the ceiling, telling himself to calm down, telling himself he was up to the challenge he faced. He'd managed a successful life after the Swenson mess. Though it had been a twenty year struggle, the guilt had not consumed him then and wouldn't after the deed was done tomorrow. He tried to remember how long it had taken for him to get some control over the initial wave of

Swenson guilt. But the memory of that period had faded; and he was too tired to work on it. He closed his eyes and tried to picture Delaney and that hair everyone mentioned. As the image of a young father with long blond hair emerged, he realized he might have two options to put the Dougie mess to bed the next day. Maybe it didn't have to be Phil. He'd just have to see what happens.

Chapter 38

When the directions from the gas station suggested Owen would be approaching the lodge, he slowed and squinted ahead for the sign that was supposed to be soon appearing on his right. On the map, the sign was huge, but Owen had to remind himself that nothing else on the map had been even remotely to scale. Even rolling along the dark road at fifteen miles an hour, he almost missed the small sign, with the words Mountain Top Lodge carved into a background of stained brown wood, like a trail marker in a national park. In fact, he did pass it at first. Couldn't read the words. But decided to back up and check because a sandy lane led off the road just beyond the sign.

He poked his car into the sandy lane about fifty yards and then had second thoughts. With no idea what to expect at the lodge and no plan for isolating Conry from Ranzone once he got there, he needed to get the lay of the land before anyone knew he was there. So he backed his car to the main road, pulled forward about one hundred yards, left the car on the shoulder, walked back to the sandy lane, and proceeded on foot to the lodge.

The lodge had to be a good mile from the main road. If not for the meager moonlight reflecting off the sandy lane, he'd have several times walked through turns directly into the forest. After ten minutes of poking his way, he could see lights among the trees ahead. He moved to the side of the sandy lane, just in case he had to jump into the tree line to avoid auto lights coming in either direction, and crept toward the lights.

Two more minutes of careful walking and he could see the lodge building clearly and, to the left, a partially lit parking area. He veered in that direction, reached the lot and crouched behind a black sedan. Though the light was weak, he could nevertheless make out a Philadelphia Government medallion attached to the rear bumper of the sedan. So, they had arrived already.

He moved from car to car until the parking lot ended at a walkway of the same sand as the lane that approached the lodge from the main road. It was well landscaped, with shrubs and small tress lining its curved route. Using the plantings as cover, he crept all the way to the lodge and knelt below a large window to a well-lit room. He could hear sounds of a football game on TV, probably the Eagles who had a Thursday night game that week. When the TV watchers erupted into cheers, he popped up and took and quick look: maybe ten men, Ranzone's age, smoking and drinking, obviously Eages fans, oblivious to anything but the replay of an Eagles score. He had only a quick look, but didn't recognixe Ranzone. Since he had never met Conry, he had no idea whether or not he was there.

From the parking lot, he had deduced that the lodge was U shaped, with the central facilities like the TV lounge and probably a dining hall at the front where he was hiding under that window, and two wings of sleeping quarters running away from each end of the main building. He slipped away from the window and headed for the left wing.

It was unlikely that Ranzone and Conry were sharing a room, but if they were, or if they were still awake and huddled together in either of their rooms, he might be able to get a look at Conry by pairing him with Ranzone whom he was sure he'd recognize. So, with a military style crawl, he moved from one window on the left wing to the next. No lights in any of the rooms. At the end of the left wing he turned and crossed an open area packed with camouflage painted four wheelers, which he assumed were used to get clients to hunting areas in the thick woods that surrounded the lodge. The open area ended with the right wing of sleeping rooms and he repeated his crawl along the outside of that wing, from one room to the next, looking for a light. There were two. Assuming—or maybe just hoping—that the inside lights would blind the occupants to what was beyond their window, that the outside world would be pitch black, he decided to brave a peek. The first room was empty but obviously occupied, with an open suitcase on the bed and a few items of clothes on the armchair. Three rooms down from that, he spotted Ranzone. He only saw his back—he was standing at his door in shorts and a tee shirt, talking to someone—but he recognized his build and his carriage immediately. He froze until he had to force himself to breathe, trying to get a glimpse of the person to whom Ranzone was speaking. Who else could it be but Conry? But he couldn't see around Ranzone's bulk. When Ranzone closed the door and turned, Owen ducked, just in case, and sat on the ground below the window. If his guess about Ranzone was correct, he had just seen a remarkable demonstration on *sang froid*, a killer nonchanantly saying goodnight to the victim he would dispatch the next day. Yet in shorts and a tee shirt, Ranzone looked like anything but a killer and Owen wondered if his convoluted theories might in fact be just a flight of fancy. Sighing, he raised himself to half-standing and crabwalked back the way he'd come until he could run unseen to the parking lot.

Chapter 39

Ranzone slept poorly. He woke repeatedly, gasping for breath, until he grabbed a cushion from the armchair in the room and slid it under the two pillows he'd already been using. But then, almost sitting up, with breathing a little easier, he wrestled with the dilemma he was facing.

Over the years, he had told himself so often that Swenson was undoubtedly guilty and Dougie maybe innocent, that he could live with his sin—if it was indeed a sin. All he'd done was remove Dougie from suspicion. While he wasn't a praying man, he found himself begging God that his coincidence idea was correct, that the real strangler decided to get out of Dodge himself. But it didn't feel like God was listening. In fact he could almost hear God laughing at him. Sure Swenson was probably guilty, God said; but so was Dougie.

Ranzone had to finally be honest with himself. He knew his brother like the back of his hand, simpleminded as he was. Had there been any real doubt about Dougie's guilt, he would never have done what he'd done. He wouldn't have felt the need. And he was now angry with himself for having put his own life and career on the line to protect Dougie. It would have been one thing if Dougie had settled into a respectful though marginal life in Florida; but that didn't seem to be the case. Homeless, refusing to communicate for years, Dougie's life since his exile to Florida had been essentially a confession to the Kensington strangings.

His thoughts were too confused to make sense of them. At one point his mind's eye fixed on a page from his grade school Bible History book, the New Testament tableau of Christ's Agony in the Garden. As the nuns had told the story that went with the picture. Jesus, being all knowing and foreseeing his crucifixion the next day, spent the night before Good Friday in the Garden of Gethsemane agonizing over the pain he knew he would have to endure. He had beseeched his Father in heaven to spare him the torture his love of mankind would require him to suffer. "Let this cup pass by me" were the words the nuns had quoted Jesus as saying. Well, that's the way Ranzone felt as he lay motionless on his bed in the darkness of his own Gethsemane. He did not want to do what he had to do; but saw no way out. He began to sob.

Yet he could not stop himself from plotting the kill shot he'd take at Phil the next day. Late afternoon would be best, with shadows distorting shapes in the woods, If he could get Phil to wander into his line of sight—or appear to have done so—the accident would be chalked up to Phil's inexperience in the woods. Maybe he would give Phil explicit instructions, in front of everyone else at the lodge, about staying clear. If it appeared that Phil had ignored his instructions, the lodge would conclude the accident was Phil's fault.

Chapter 40

By the time Owen reached his parked car, the fall mountain air was chilling the sweat gatherd on his back. And his clothes were spotted with dirt from his crawl around the lodge. He could not remember passing a motel on his way from the Interstate, so he continued on the unnamed lodge road for about a half hour until drowziness overcame him. Except for periods of unconsciousness in that shed on the beach, he had not rested at all the night before. So he pulled off into a small picnic area along the road, layered on the clothes from his night bag as best he could, tilted his seat back and slept, shivering himself awake every few minutes, until sunrise.

When the sounds of vehicles passing on the road woke him to the half tones of dawn, Owen struggled out of the car, stretched, took a leak against a tree and then headed back in the direction he had come. On the way, he stopped at another gas station/convenience store and bought a micrwaved breakfast sandwich and coffee, then continued on to the lodge.

When he reached the sandy lane, he stopped, uncertain whether to drive or walk the rest of the way. He checked his watch. Eight AM. With any luck, most of the hunters would be out already and he could reach the parking lot without being noticed. Not only that, but he was not really in danger. Conry was. And in the worse case scenario, he'd just ask to speak to him privately. Tell him the Dougie story and leave the decision up to him. So he drove up the lane and in a couple of minutes was in the parking lot, parked next to Ranzone's sedan. He slumped down in his seat and waited. No one bothered him and as the sun hit his windshield and warmed the car, he dozed off until a vague dream of a grizzled hunter aiming a rifle at him from about ten feet way startled him awake. He sat up and looked around. There had obviously not yet been an accident. No commotion, no ambulance, no police. But the day was young.

He got out of the car, still bulked up with layers of shirts and underwear, and stole his way to the lodge. When the lean man with a multi pocked vest and a military bearing came out the front door to raise the flag on a twenty foot flagpole, Owen hid behind an oversized SUV. When the man returned inside, Owen rushed along the left wing of the lodge to the woods behind it from where he could watch the comings and goings of the camouflaged four-wheelers in the space between the building wings. There were two left. He sat behind a large tree and waited. At about nine, the flag raiser, now wearing a bright orange vest, entered the four-wheeler lot through a back door of the main building and hopped on one of the two vehicles. He started it up without apparently inserting a key and pulled off into the woods to Owen's left. Owen strained to hear sounds from inside the lodge. He thought he could hear kitchen sounds, but nothing else. So, anticipating that he would just ask for Phil Conry if he were stopped, he walked casually to the remaining four-wheeler to see if it had a key. It did. He walked back to his hideout in the woods and sat to wait, certain he hadn't been noticed.

At about eleven thirty, he heard the roar of a four-wheeler returning to the lodge. Then another, and another. Like sea birds returning to their rookery. Time for lunch. By eleven forty-five, the four-wheeler lot was almost full and rifles had been set into gun racks on the outside wall of the main building. But no sign of Ranzone and Conry. Owen worried that he'd been too late, that Conry was already dead and Ranzone would soon be racing in alone to report the accident. His heart thumped as he waited for the growling sound of a four-wheeler approaching the lodge; and he exhaled sharpley and almost stood up to cheer when he saw Ranzone approaching with a rider on the back end of the generous seat of his vehicle. Unlike the other hunters, neither Ranzone nor Conry were wearing the typical orange vests or hats. There was something orange stuffed between them, however; so maybe they had taken their protective outfits off when they started back to the lodge. But curious nevertheless. The two men dismounted, hung their rifles and went in to eat.

Owen had not thought to buy something for lunch and he was hungry. But not hungry enough to go get something and take a chance on missing Ranzone and Conry leave for what he presumed would be an afternoon hunt. He assumed Conry and Ranzone would separate when they were in the woods, so he planned to take that last four-wheeler and follow Ranzone and Conry and then close in on Conry when they had gone their own ways. Then he would warn Conry of the danger he might be in. On the other hand, if Conry and Ranzone stayed close together, he would take the chance of approaching them together and try to tell Conry his story. In that event Ranzone would shout that Owen was insane; but Owen's presence would at least offer Conry protection until after the hunt. As he envisioned the scary afternoon, he found himself hoping that his suspicions of Ranzone were just another fantasy.

When the hunters emerged from lunch, they stood around barking insults at each other or wishing each other better luck in the afternoon session. Sounded like not a single one of them had shot a deer that morning. Above the chatter, Owen could make out Ranzone's voice telling Conry to be more careful when they went back out.

"Always stay in your assigned area. You crept into my line of sight this morning. It can be dangerous to get in anyone's line of sight."

Owen watched as the hunters left, marking the route in which Ranzone headed, again with Conry riding behind. They had not put on their colorful clothes. The flag raiser was the last to leave, with his own rifle set in the long holster attached to his four-wheeler. When there was again only one four-wheeler left, Owen walked to it, sat down and studied the controls. He had ridden a jet ski on several occasions at the Jersey shore and it didn't take long to figure out that the operations were similar.

The four-wheeler fired up when he pressed the start button and he gently twisted the hand throttle, rolling out of the lot slowly and picking up speed as he hit the trail Ranzone had taken.

Chapter 41

Conry had enjoyed the morning hunt, much to his surprise. He had not seen any deer, to his relief, but liked walking the woods for a couple of hours. The lodge hunting ground was divided into pie shaped sectors by the four-wheeler trails running spokelike from the lodge itself. A diagram on the wall of the dining hall indicated that each of those spokes was about three quarters of a mile long and Ranzone had stopped about half way along their trail to give a brief lesson on how to operate his rifle, to advise Conry not to wear his orange vest since deer had learned to associate that bright color with gunfire, and to instruct Conry to face back toward the lodge and treat that section as his. Ranzone took the wider portion of the pie extending away from the lodge and headed for what he called a deer stand, a low walled, wooden platform about twenty feet off the ground wedged between the twin trunks of a huge oak. When Conry turned back to look, he had seen Ranzone struggle up an ancient wooden ladder to reach the stand which was camouflaged with dejected looking branches ripped from the nearby foliage. The effort was almost painful to watch and, when Conry returned to the tree for their scheduled lunch break, he worried that Ranzone would fall on his climb back down. And, in fact, when he returned to the tree after his morning stroll, Conry was dismayed by Ranzone's halting creep down the ladder, it took Ranzone a few minutes of heavy breathing, sitting on the fourwheeler, before he patted the back seat for Conry to climb on and ride back to the lodge with him.

Despite anxieties about Ranzone's condition, Conry was looking forward to the afternoon session. Ranzone drove about the same distance along their four-wheeler trail; but said he was going to forego the deer blind and hunt from the ground. The climb up and down was too much for him. He'd use the four-wheeler to rest if he needed it. So he wove the four-wheeler, Conry sitting behind him, to the vicinity of the deer stand. Ranzone stopped, dismounted, wished Conry luck and sent him on his way back to his area between the tree and the lodge.

Conry did not even bother to load his rifle but figured he'd wander the woods for a couple hours again, enjoying the almost haunted aspect of the partially denuded forest, kicking through the carpet of leaves like a kid, and return to the tree stand area at four when Ranzone said he wanted to head back.

Real fatigue made Ranzone's excuses about foregoing the deer blind a believable reason to move about on foot. No one would know how he and Conry had divided their sector and all he had to do was creep back toward the lodge on Conry's tail until he was close enough and Conry was open enough for a kill shot. His chest heaved, a discomfort he put down to anxiety about what he knew he was going to do. But the trudge through the woods, climbing over fallen trees, jumping little rivulets and backing aside branches blocking his way, left him wobbly. He stopped frequently to sit on the ground or a downed tree trunk, making his progress toward Conry slower than he'd expected. He had waited nearly fifteen minutes at the deer stand to give Conry enough of a head start that he wouldn't notice him following behind. But Conry had to be moving faster than he was. When he could still not see him after a few minutes, he picked up his pace.

The faster pace was hard for Ranzone. He told himself that the lack of exercise during the campaign was taking his toll, as were the many huge meals he had cheerfully endured to please potential voters or local pols. Although he had not felt like eating much at lunch, and in fact only picked at his food, he was feeling nauseous as he plodded toward Conrey. It was an odd sensation, hunting a human being, stalking him like he was a creature of the forest. And he wanted to get it over with as soon as possible. His agony of conscience of the previous night had passed. He was confident, almost exhilarated, that it would all work out. And, as for the looming guilt, he told himself that, like a relentless river watering down jagged stone into rounded boulders, time would be his friend. It had dulled the sharpness of the Swenson mess to the point where, until that Delaney came poking around, he could for long stretches of time actually make himself forget it had happened. And the same would happen with the Phil problem. Things were falling into place. Delaney had never showed up at the lodge; and Phil had suspected nothing, and had even stupidly fell for the line about the orange vest. And once Phil was gone, he could tell Shapiro to go to hell.

He had hoped to bag a deer as the final coup of the campaign, and when he saw a four-point buck steak across his line of vision, he started to follow it. But after thirty breathless seconds, he gave up. Not only was the effort too much, but he remembered the special season was for antlerless deer only. And he told himself the original, innocent, if cynical, political plan was no longer the priority. He listened for gunshots from Conry. Sometimes when a buck crosses your path, more of the herd is nearby. But he heard nothing. Indeed all afternoon he'd heard only a few scattered shots from other sectors. Maybe no one would get anything and his own failure would not be noteworthy.

After hesitating over the buck, he knew he had to hurry. Conry would not walk all the way back to the lodge and as he got closer to it, their sector narrowed and he would probably turn back. He had to get him in sight before then.

Struggling with the hillier terrain in Conry's portion of their sector, he pushed forward with his legs growing heavier and his chest tightening. Eventually, with great effort, he crested a small hill and, once he could see beyond it, spotted Conry. He was talking to a younger man in a light blue shirt. With striking blond hair.

Chapter 42

Owen had driven his four-wheeler slowly along the trail that Ranzone had taken. He stopped frequently to listen for sounds, anything, talking or even gunshots; and heard nothing but the wind and the birds. He had a sense from the pattern of four-wheeler routes over which the hunters had dispersed that the hunting ground was divided into sectors by the trails themselves, but he did not know whether the Ranzone/Conry sector was to his right or left of the trail they had taken. He dismounted after a careful three minutes and proceeded on foot, searching both sides for a glimpse of hunter orange. After about one hundred and fifty yards, he saw Conry to his right. Or at least he thought it was Conry, no orange vest, sitting on a fallen tree, watching a line of wild turkeys quick step away from him.

Worried that he himself might become the victim of a real hunting accident, he was apprehensive about approaching the sitting figure. And once again, he realized how foolish his message to Conry would seem. To deal with the first worry, he stripped off his blood stained sport coat, exposing a blue dress shirt which he thought would look less like a deer to Conry, and walked directly toward him, waving the coat above his head as he did. As to the second worry, he'd just have to take his chances and hope that if Ranzone did in fact have murder on his mind, Owen's presence would give him pause.

When he was thirty yards from Conry, Owen began to whistle like a large blue chested brown bird chirping in the forest. Conry looked up. Owen waved his sportcoat frantically. Conry noticed, stood and walked toward him.

Owen called out "Phil Conry?"

"Yes." He looked worried and hurried to get closer. "Everything all right? My family?"

"There all fine, Mr. Conry." Owen exhaled heavily. "But I have to talk to you about your boss. You may be in danger."

Conry wrinkled his nose and said "Who are you?"

"My name is Owen Delaney. We've spoken on the phone a couple of times about the Swenson case."

Conry squinted. "And?"

Owen didn't want to go into chapter and verse of his armchair detective work, so he cut to the chase. "I don't think Swenson was the Kennsington Strangler. Ranzone's brother Dougie was the Strangler. Ranzone planted that obsidianite to shift suspicion to Swenson. And you're the only one who knows he did it."

"I know no such thing. What are you talking about?"

"Why do you think he suddenly wanted you on this hunting trip?"

That gave Conry pause. He turned to look back over his shoulder, then faced Owen and said "Go on. I'm listening."

Owen hurried to the little clearing where Conry had stopped to watch those turkeys, where he could talk to him without shouting. He tried to explain that Ranzone suspected his brother of the stranglings, planted the obsidianite to make Swenson look guilty of them, and sent his brother out of town to make the stranglings stop. But Conry looked more and more skeptical as he went along, particularly when Owen described the trail of similar stranglings that followed Dougie wherever he went in Florida.

"I think you're crazy."

"I'd be happy if I was. But I had to warn you to be careful. You might be the victim of—"

A shot rang out and Owen could hear a snap of the bark breaking off a nearby tree. They both looked in the direction of the gunshot and saw Ranzone, standing on the crest of a small hill with his gun raised for a second shot. Conry pushed Owen toward the nearest tree and threw himself in the opposite direction behind another tree. Shots kept ringing out and Owen could hear them strike the ground or the trees behind which he and Conry were taking cover. Maybe Ranzone didn't care which of the two of them he killed. Crazy. Foolish. The shooting had to convince Conry that something was off. So if he himself were shot, Conry would know what Owen had told him was true. If Conry was killed, it would be Ranzone's word aginst Owen's. Ranzone should be aiming only for Conry.

As he stood with his back up against his protecting tree, Owen concluded that, as hard as it would be to describe what had happened as an accident, Ranzone would probably try to shoot both of them and make up some tragic accident story afterwards. After all, what motive could he have had for cold-blooded murder? So this was it for Owen? Death by good intentions.

Owen looked over at Conry who made a calm down gesture with his hands and snuck a peak around his tree. Another shot popped and the leaves about five feet from Conry's tree rustled with the impact of the bullet. Ranzone's aim was deteriorating. So Owen braved a peek himself and could see Ranzone staggering around on the hilltop. When he saw Owen's head, he lifted his rifle to shoot but the shot came some seconds after Owen was safely behind his tree. And the shot landed maybe ten feet from Owen.

Conry had left his rife propped against a fallen tree about ten feet from the tree behind which he was now hiding; and when Owen pointed to it, Conry shook his head and whispered "It's unloaded." So firing back at Ranzone was impossible without Conry exposing himself to gunfire as he fetched and loaded his rifle. But something was wrong with Ranzone's aim. The first shots he took had been close to their targets, but each successive one was further and further off the mark. Owen worried that Ranzone would walk down the hill for a closer shot. He said Conry, "Should we run for it?"

"You take a four-wheeler out here?"

"Yeah, its about one hundred yards down the trail." Owen pointed to the trail he had taken.

"Okay. Spread apart. Weave your way to the trail and run like hell to the four-wheeler. On three. . . one . . . two . . . three."

The two men ran in serpentine patterns toward the trail, jumping fallen trees and, splashing through little creeks along the fifty yards to the trail. For some reason, despite the fact that he'd probably never wear that sport coat again, Owen swung it along with him as he ran. No shots followed them. When they reached the trail they sprinted toward the four-wheeler. Conry took the front seat and made an expert three-point turn and headed back to the lodge. All was quiet behind them.

Chapter 43

Ranzone's rifle had gotten heavier by the minute. The climb up the little hill from which he had the view of Conry and Delaney—indeed, even the trudge from the four-wheeler which he'd left at the base of the deer stand tree—had exhausted him. His left arm ached as he lifted his rifle to aim and he felt like his chest was collapsing. Though he *could* breathe, he felt like breathing should be impossible with the tightness in his chest. When Conry and Delaney ducked behind trees, he debated going down the hill for a closer shot but the effort seemed too much. So he decided to wait them out.

With each minute of wait, he felt more lightheaded. Something was wrong with him. He felt clammy and was overcome with an undefined sense of dread. But he shakily stood his ground. When Conry poked his head out for a look, he aimed his rifle and pulled the trigger. But the reflex was executed in slow motion. Same when Delaney's head appeared for a second. He could not focus on anything but his own chest. He felt faint and wobbled as he stood watch. He was desperate. He knew he had to get both of them now. His mind was too clouded to figure out how he'd explain it afterward, but his whole world depended on his success. He'd work on the story when they were dead.

After minutes during which all of them were frozen in an eerie tableau, Delaney and Conry bolted from behind their trees and began a wild scramble. Back toward the lodge. Ranzone tried to raise his rifle to shoot but could not even lift it. He realized he no longer cared.

"Damn. Let them go" he said to himself, and flopped down on the crunchy leaves and laid his rifle beside him.

PART IV
THE MESSY AFTERMATH

Chapter 44

When Conry and Owen reached the lodge, there was no one there other than the kitchen staff preparing the next meal. Conry asked for a phone and they directed him to Michael's office. Apparently, Michael was the military style director of the lodge opertions Owen had noticed wearing that the multi pocketd vest. Once in Michael's office, Conry grabbed the desk phone to call 911. But Owen held up a cautionary palm.

"What do we say just happened? Do we accuse the next governor of trying to kill us? Just like that?"

Conry put the phone down and sat in Michael's chair with a stunned look. "You're right. Maybe we should just report some unusual shooting out in the woods, shooting that didn't sound like hunters."

"Right. Let them come and figure out what happened. So we don't sound like we're deranged."

By the time the single sheriff's patrol car pulled up the sandy lane about twenty minutes later, a few of the other hunters had returned and had shuffled to their rooms to shower without asking for John. The sheriff was dubious as Conry explained that the shooting activity he'd heard was unusual, that some of it came dangerously close to him. He suggested the two of them ride out to the shooting area to investigate. He did not mention that Owen had been with him and Owen settled into the background to listen, still worried for Conry's safety. But he called Conry to his side before Conry left with the sheriff and asked if Conry thought he should stick around. Would that complicate or simplify things? Conry shifted his weight from one foot to the other for a few second and said "If John denies the shooting, it would be good for you to be here. Otherwise it would be my word against his. So stay. Wait till we get back and see what happens."

Ranzone was dead when they found him. The sheriff's deputy checked him for signs of gunshot wounds or othet violence but found none. He suggested that he had suffered a heart attack. Conry wasn't surprised. John had not looked well for a while and had not been himself the previous day. So, out of respect for his friend and boss, he decided to say nothing about Ranzone's attempt to kill him and Delaney.

They left Ranzone in the woods and returned slowly to the lodge where the sheriff called an ambulance and the medical examiner. Conry told Owen what they had found and said "Maybe you should go. I don't have my phone with me, but you should call me late tomorrow when we know more and can figure out what do do."

Owen hurried to his rental car and drove away with a racing heart that did not slow down until he was almost home.

The medics rolled a gurney out to a point on the fourwheeler trail near where Ranzone lay, then carried him from the woods back to the gurney and wheeled him to the lodge. The last bit of their journey to the ambulance resembled a tribute to a fallen hero, with all the old hunters standing aside, heads bowed respectfully.

Conry stayed the night at the lodge, after calling Elizabeth and the party chairman, and waiting for the medical examiner's report which arrived in the morning. As they all expected, the examiner had found that Ranzone had suffered a heart attack and died alone on that hill. Conry then made arrangements for the transport of the body to Philadelphia. It was now Saturday and the election was Tuesday. He had no idea what he should do next and his drive back to Philadelphia was a very slow one indeed.

Chapter 45

Though it took him out of his way, Owen drove to the rental return lot at Philadelphia International rather than head straight home. He was apprehensive about facing Barbara, sure his traumatic experiences had left a mark but unsure whether that mark was clear enough for Barbara to notice. He had deceived Barbara in incremental steps throughout his big adventure, though he had not yet told an outright lie. But taking public transportation back to Chestnut Hill from the airport, he realized that although the news about Ranzone would be all over the news, Barbara did not know that Ranzone and his brother were the focus of his armchair detective work. Except for the wound on his head, nothing should give Barb any anxiety over what happened on his trip. If and when she noticed it, he would tell her he had hit his head putting his bag into the trunk of the rental car. Maybe his hair was long enough to hide the neat little bandage.

He arrived home about ten thirty. He had stuffed his bloody sportcoat into his overnight bag and was cold when he came in the back door. Barb said he was crazy for going without a jacket but, otherwise, she greeted him warmly . When asked about the bandage on his head, he gave her the rehearsed story about hitting his head while closing the trunk of his rental. Then he quickly asked about the kids and if there was anything good to eat. Barb gave him a beef stew to microwave and went back to the TV while he prepared it.

No sooner had the TV lit up than a news bulletin about Ranzone's death from a probable heart attack while engaging in his favorite pastime flashed on the screen. TV crews were all over the Mountain Top lodge, interviewing hunters and staff. Owen was happy he hadn't stayed around; but remembered he'd told Barbara that he'd be in the Poconos for two days and checked her out of the corner of his eye to see if she was giving him any inquisitive looks. He didn't detect any; but thought he should register great surprise at the mention of the Lodge, just in case. "My God, I was there today. Went to talk to the lead detective in the Swenson case. He was hunting with Ranzone. I left before all the commotion."

At that point, Barb did look puzzled. "Why did you have to go up there to talk to him, if he's a Philadelphia detective."

Owen swallowed hard. "I was anxious to check out a hunch that developed in Florida. I guess I could've waited, but I didn't."

"Well, did the hunch check out?"

"Yes, I think so."

"Good." Barb turned her attention back to the TV but Owen couldn't concentrate on it. His stomach churned from his deceptions to Barbara. And more that that, though his trip to the Poconos had definitely confirmed his hunch about Ranzone, he didn't see how he could use his discovery without keying Barbara in to his harrowing adventure. And even worse, now that his hero Ranzone was dead, he didn't think Conry would tell his tale just to help Swenson, whom he thought was guilty in the first place.

On Sunday about five, Owen called Conry and made arrangements to meet for lunch the following day at a cafe across from the Ranzone campaign headquarters on Broad Street. When Owen arrived, Conry was already seated at a corner booth. He looked exhausted.

"You okay?" Owen asked as he slid into the booth across from Conry.

"Not really." Conry shook his head and sighed. "Couldn't eat. Just ordered coffee." He looked down to his still full cup, then picked his head up and said "I've known John almost all of my adult life. I want to be angry at him, but it's hard. I couldn't even tell my wife what happened." He sighed again. "I'm very sad."

"I understand. For what it's worth, I didn't tell my wife either. But it's gonna have to come out sooner or later."

"Why? Why can't we let it rest in peace? That would be best for John's family. And to accuse his brother of the Kennsington Stranglings would only make matters worse for them. Unless you've got some do-gooder notion that the brother should be brought to trial."

"The brother's dead."

"All the more reason to let it lie."

"But what about Swenson?"

"What about him?"

"I think there's a good chance he's innocent."

"I doubt that."

"Maybe. But my do-gooder streak is pushing me to try and get his case opened. I really think he was convicted only because Ranzone was able to make everyone think he was the Strangler."

"Yeah. But Strangler or not, he was guilty of the murder we put him away for. At least I still think so."

"But suppose he wasn't."

Owen went through the particulars of case again for Conry, reminding him that Phelan's testimony was more or less contradicted by his wife, that the Phillies game alibi was pretty good, and that the only piece of evidence that he hadn't been able to challenge was the testimony of Greg Stuart about seeing Swenson cleaning his knife which, he pointed out again, was highly questionable. No residue of blood was found on the knife or in the boarding house sink.

"And you think dragging John's reputation through the mud is gonna help Swenson?"

"I think so."

"But how?" Conry tapped his figers on the table. "I'll admit that it sure seems like John planted that piece of coal to throw us off the track that might lead to his brother. His trying to kill me—and you—is probably proof of that. But it doesn't mean that Swenson is innocent. So John's dead brother was the Strangler. So what, if Swenson killed that bingo lady."

"Well, I'm gonna work to get the Swenson case reopened." Owen tried to look Conry in the eyes but could not catch them. "If I'm successful and the judge permits testimony about that Apache Tear, will you tell the court what you told me? That John was the one to find it. Days after the murder."

"I wouldn't lie. But I'd have a hard time testifying."

"Fair enough. I'll keep you informed."

After leaving Conry still staring at his coffee, Owen walked over to Market Street and strolled down to the building where the Innocence Project was located. He wondered if Glassman had given any credence at all to Owen' belief that Ranzone had falsely created the impression that Swenson was the Strangler?

He had no appointment with Glassman; so, to soften the surprise, he called from the street out side the building. Glassman must have been unoccupied, since whoever answered the phone put Owen through immediately.

"Bob? Owen Delaney here." He paused and said "I'd like to talk to you some more about John Ranzone."

"I suppose you know he died over the weekend. What a mess that makes. For the election, I mean."

"I'm sure it does; but I wanted to talk about about him and the Swenson case."

"You think now that Ranzone's dead you can make a stronger case against him?"

"No. Now that I've learned more about him, I know I can make a stronger case."

"Okay, I guess I can give you a few minutes. When should we do it?"

"How 'bout right now. I'm downstairs."

It was impossible for Owen to make his case without going into all the details about his Florida trip, his worry for Conry, and Ranzone's attempt to kill both him and Conry at the hunting lodge just before he had his heart attack. Glassman made faces throughout the story. When Owen finished Glassman sighed and said "Why can't it all be more simple? Give me some DNA evidence anytime over a story like yours."

"It can't be simple because it's a complicated story. But I think you should pursue it anyway. There may not be any need to bring Ranzone into it. Most of the convicting evidence was circumstantial and can easily be challenged. But if my Ranzone story is essential, Detective Conry is willing to testify."

That last bit roused Glassman. He leaned back in his recliner and said "the biggest problem as I see it is that the complexity is probably too much for our current staff to handle. Sure, they could prepare motions to challenge that circumstantial evidence. But getting the significance of the Ranzone angle to a judge or jury without a full-blown scandal would be tricky. Probably beyond any of our young guys. And frankly, as administrator of the office, I'm not the man for the job either."

Owen thought and then said "Suppose I find someone a little more experienced than your young staff to take the case pro-bono?"

"Go for it."

Owen could not get a meeting with Peter Martin until Wednesday. Martin had been in court on a personl injury case. By the time Wednesday arrived, with there having been no time to change the ballots or promote a write-in candidate, the dead John Ranzone had been elected Governor; his running mate, a lawyer from Clearfield County, had beeeen elected Lieutenant

Governor, and the guest experts on the TV news had been analyzing the consequences of the election to death, so to speak.

It was still unclear who would be the next governor and how that would happen. The death of a candidate before an election was certified was a rarity. But it had happened, even once after a Presidential election. In that case, electors in the electoral college had to switch their sixty-six votes from Horace Greely, who had died after the election, to Ulysses S. Grant. And it had happened more often in state elections. Even where the deceased party had been the winner of the election. In those instances, the governor of the state was typically able to appoint a temporary replacement and then call a special election for the office of the deceased candidate.

If the deceased were the governor elect, would the incumbent governor simply remain in office until a special election was held? Most pundits said yes; that would be the solution in that case. But the death of a candidate before the election, so close to the date of the election that ballots couldn't be changed beforehand, was another matter. Had Ranzone lost the election, there would have been no problem But he won. What happens then? The question then becomes, do the votes cast for the deceased actually count? If they don't, does that mean his opponent has won? Or should his running mate be named governor? According to the experts, the state election code appeared to require the existing governor to call for a special election, and the code mandated that the special election be held at least ninety days after the disputed election. Adhering to that schedule would mean that the special election would be held some time after the governor's term expired. So, who would then be governor? Would the governor's term be extended, in which case he'd have no incentive to call the spcial election? Or would the elected lieutenant governor succeed to the deceased governor elect's responsibilities?

Selecting Ranzone's successor as District Attorney was a relatively easy matter. The Common Pleas Court Board of Judges selected one of Ranzone's long time assistants to be the interim DA until the victorious Democratic candidate in the recent election took office.

Martin had a small TV on in his office when Owen arrived. He turned the volume down when his paralegal escorted Owen into the office, but couldn't fully take his attention away from the talking heads. Owen was curious about the legal niceties of the gubenatorial sucession too, but he had to remind Martin that he had come to discuss the Swenson case.

"As I told you on the phone, since we last spoke, I've become convinced that Swenson was railroaded." That was essentially all Owen had said when he asked for the meeting. But then, just in case Martin assumed Owen was there simply to comfort him, Owen said "And I'd like to recruit you to help him."

Martin turned down the volume on his television.

Owen went on. "What I'm about to tell you is confidential and, unless the Swenson case gets opened, it is probably unproveable because the key witness is reluctant to speak up unless he's forced to under oath."

"Uh, huh." Martin looked skeptical, and he snuck a look at the TV. So Owen went straight to the bottom line. "John Ranzone framed Charles Swenson."

Martin clicked off the TV and leaned forward. "Tell me more," he said.

Owen gave him chapter and verse, including the work he'd done that corroborated the Philles game alibi and challenged the Phelan testimony, and including Ranzone's efforts to prevent him from finding his brother in Florida.

"And what about the testimony of that fellow in the rooming house about Swenson cleaning his knife the night of the murder?"

"I've talked to him and couldn't shake his story; but I don't believe it."

"Why's that?"

"Too perfect. Too incriminating. I noticed you didn't cross examine him aggressively."

"That's true. I was wary of his piling on my cient. Are you saying Ranzone had him perjure himself?"

"No. But by creating the impression that Swenson was the Kennsington Strangler, it was almost like putting words in his mouth."

Owen said nothing more for a full thirty seconds. Martin stared at his hands. Finally, Owen said "I think you have a chance to redeem yourself. You're a more experienced trial lawyer now. How often do you get a chance to go back and redo the poor performaces of your youth?"

"Who would pay me? The Innocence Project?"

"No. They can't afford that. I'm thinking pro bono."

Martin hung his head. "Like I can afford to work for free." He waved his arm around his small, messy office.

"I could help you. I went to law school and passed the PA bar. And I'm a licensed private detective besides. And I know the details in and out."

"That's unfair. You're taking advantage of my holdover guilt about the case."

"That's my general strategy. Yes. Can you think of anyone better to ask?"

"I don't know. Let me think about it."

Chapter 46

Shapiro wanted to get paid. He had called John Rogers answering service a half dozen times without a call back. While he knew John Rogers true identity, he had not heard about Ranzone's death. He rarely watched the news, what with Sports Center on at all hours. So he called Calderone and learned that Ranzone had died of a heart attack, just days before. He didn't believe him at first, thinking maybe Ranzone had paid Calderone for both of their efforts and Calderone had kept it all. He could easily believe that of Mike. So he checked the Internet and confirmed Calderone's story; but the reports of a heart attack were too pat. He was suspicious. Ranzone had been involved in something shady and his death had to be connected to that. He'd read that a heart attack could be induced with chemicals and wondered if someone had gotten to Ranzone. Or maybe he'd been killed some other way and his political pals were just covering it up with the heart attack story. How the hell could he figure out if that was the case? And what good would it do him to find out, unless of course he could threaten to expose Ranzone's murder or the pols who were covering up.

He called Calderone to try out his theory. Calderone listened but reminded Shapiro that Ranzone was in his sixties, so a natural heart attack was plausible. And besides, even assuming someone had killed Ranzone, how would they figure out who did it. And if they did, would the murderers be afraid of a little blackmail or would they just give him and Shapiro their own heart attacks.

By now, Shapiro was back at the Villages and sagged in his plump TV armchair at the thought of returning to Miami to continue the search for Ranzone's brother who had to be the key to the Ranzone murder. He didn't like Miami at all. But he did know where to find the only other person he knew who had been involved in Ranzone's mystery. His contact in Philly knew exactly where that Owen Delaney lived and he, himself, knew exactly what he looked like. If he was correct in his hunch, finding Ranzone's killer might be worth more than Ranzone's unpaid bill.

Chapter 47

On Friday, Owen received a call from Peter Martin telling him he'd take the Swenson case, pro bono, but only if Owen could find a way to impeach Greg Stuart's testimony about the knife cleaning. Martin thought that was enough to convict even if they were unable to create reasonable doubt about Phelan's testimony and the Phillies game. Owen agreed to try; and went through his notes for Stuart's cell phone number. When he reached Stuart they agreed to meet at Barkley's on Friday night.

The crowd at Barkleys was again thin, and old, and Owen wondered how the bar continued to survive. Friday night and no more than eight people in the place, including himself. Dying like the Avenue but determined to preserve its old role as the neighborhood watering hole. He almost laughed at the reception he imagined young junkies from the area getting if they dared set foot in the place.

Stuart was sitting at a table with three other men, all in their late fifties or early sixties. He apparently recognized Owen from their earlier meeting and waved at him to come over and sit. Owen approached the table but didn't sit.

"Do you think we should talk privately, Mr. Stuart?"

Stuart shrugged and shook his head. "No need. These guys are all my friends. They knew Charles as well as I did. And Jimmy Phelan too. So ask away."

Owen had decided that he would at least suggest to Stuart that Swenson was not the Strangler. That there was evidence to prove it was someone else; that that someone was now dead. But that seemed a big step to take with Stuart's friends sitting around the table. He sat down anyway.

"Nice to see you again, Greg. The reason I wanted to talk is that since we last spoke I've learned that some of the convicting evidence against Charles turns out be have been weaker than his lawyer at the time thought. We're hoping to get a new trial."

Owen went into the details of Phelan's wife's contradiction of at least parts of his testimony, and the finding of the Phillies ticket and the late ending of the game. The audience around the table sat stonefaced until Stuart spoke up.

"Yeah. Maybe. But I seen him cleaning that knife. I'm sure of that. What do you make of that piece of evidence?"

"All I can ask is 'are you sure?' I think that knife business is the only thing that a jury would wonder about if Charles got a new trial."

"And why the hell should they give a new trial to the Strangler? I wouldn't give him the time of day." The others at the table murmured their agreement.

Owen took a deep breath. He would love to tell the full story; but the truth would probably not be as believable as their conviction that Swenson was the Strangler. He hoped his old standby, the partial truth, would work. "You know, Charles wasn't the Strangler. The Strangler died a couple of years ago in Florida."

"How do you know that?"

"Let's just say it can be proved; but it would be embarrassing to the people who put Charles away. They never accused him of being the Strangler, you know. Just let everybody think so. But even so, Charles is in prison for the murder of that bingo lady, not the stranglings, and if he didn't do that, he should be a free man."

One of Stuart's buddies spoke up. "But suppose he did do that?"

"Well, I don't think he did. That's why it's important that you be sure Greg saw him cleaning that knife when he says he saw him. Remember the cops never found any blood in his room or in the bathroom where Greg thinks he saw him washing it."

Stuart twisted his lips and squinted. Then he scanned the grizzled group sitting around the table. Owen noticed a few raised eyebrows and shoulders lifted infinitisemally. Finally, Stuart said "Let me think about it. Charles wasn't a bad guy and he's an old man like us now."

Owen slid one of Peter Martin's cards across the table to Stuart. "If you remember anything differently, call him." He pointed to Martin's number. "He's Charles lawyer."

"And who are you? I thought you was the lawyer."

"No. I'm a lawyer but I'm working for Charles more as an investigator. For Charles and the Innocence Project. That's an organization that tries to free up innocent persons who've been convicted of crimes, particularly serious crimes like murder."

"Innocent?" Stuart snorted a short laugh. But he took Martin's card.

Chapter 48

By the following Tuesday, the governor elect matter had been settled by the bureau in the Pennsylvania Secretary of State's office which had jurisdiction over election matters. The Bureau's conclusion was that Tom Wade, elected Lieutenant Governor in the recent election, would be installed as the next governor of Pennsylvania. He said all the right things to the news media: tragic loss, would do his best to fill a big pair of shoes, would depend on the support of the good people of Pennsylnavia, etc, etc. But Owen sensed that he was trembling inside.

Owen wondered whether Conry had felt obliged to tell someone, somewhere, about Ranzone's framing of Swenson. And he needed to speak to Conry about the partial, though indirect, disclosure of their secret to Greg Stuart. So, Owen called Conry.

"Phil? May I call you Phil?"

"Sure. How're you doing? Owen?"

"Yeah, Owen's fine." Owen paused. "I called to let you know that I spoke to Greg Stuart. You remember him? The guy who says he saw Swenson cleaning his knife."

"Says he saw? As I recall, he was pretty convincing. It expained why there was no blood on the knife."

"I remember. But when I told him Swenson was not the Strangler, he softened a bit."

"What exactly did you tell him? You didn't mention John, I hope."

"No. Just told him there was proof. Thought you should know. Just in case he asks for that proof. Have you told anyone about John?"

"No, and I don't intend to unless my testimony is supoenaed. Is that why you're calling me?"

"No. I hope it doesn't come to that. But I thought you should know that at least part of the story is out there."

Conry didn't speak and Owen bit his lip until Conry finally said "Well, thanks for telling me. But don't expect me to get all co-operative just because you couldn't hold you own tongue."

"I understand, Phil. Let's hope we can do it all without you."

"Better believe it."

Owen was in his home office when Shapiro called.

"Professor Delany, nice to speak to you again."

Owen got goosebumps at the sound of that harsh New York accent but said nothing in response.

"Professor, don't be shocked. You're not that hard to find. My boys got your cell phone number from your secretary at the University. She said you was on sabbatical, or something like that. Funny, with that hair, I would never have taken you for Jewish. But she was very helpful."

The caller's ignorance irritated Owen. "Sabbatical is just an academic term for leave of absence. Has nothing to do with the Sabbath."

"Okay. Okay. But I didn't call to learn any new words. I called to ask for money."

"Money?"

"Yeah. The way I figure it you had something to do with John Ranzone's death. And naturally wouldn't want anybody to know about it."

"That's crazy. Ranzone died of a heart attack. Check the news."

"I did; but you and I know he was involved in something fishy down here. That's why you was snooping around. I never believed his story 'bout trying to hide his drunken brother. Him and his brother, and probably you, had to be involved in something bigger than that. Either you pay me to forget all about it or you tell me Ranzone's secret. I'll take it from there."

Owen had a flash of mischievous thought. If he told the New York voice about Ranzone, and the New Yorker couldn't find anyone in the campaign to blackmail over it—and who could he find who'd believe it enough to pay—he might go public. And that would help Swenson. But that was unconscionable. Probably. He let the idea roll around in his head for while.

After a half minute, the caller said "You still there, Professor?"

"Yeah, just thinking."

"Well, don't think too hard, or too long. You got my number. If I don't hear from you, I'll get back to you. Say a week?"

Owen grunted but said "Just wondering. How much money you think this craziness is worth?"

"Let's say twenty five grand."

Owen sat at his desk in a daze for a long time after his call with the New Yorker ended. Even if the caller had said he wanted a hundred dollars, he would refuse to pay. What he really wanted was for the caller to go public with the Ranzone story. Once it was out there, the case for Swenson would strengthen. But telling him about Ranzone would be hard, and wrong, even if he did it only to help Swenson. He had promised Conry. And not only that, the real story would let Barbara know that his Swenson work hadn't been a walk in the park, the impression he had worked so hard and so deceitfully to create.

The more he thought about it, keeping Barbara in the dark was more important than the promise he'd made to Conry. After all, what kind of promise was that. A promise to help save the reputation of his friend, a man who had framed poor Charles Swenson and let him sit in prison for years. Why did that reputation deserve protection? So how could he tell the New Yorker the truth and not alarm Barbara? And if he did tell him the truth, did that mean he'd leave Owen alone. And his family? And his reputation?

By the time he got up from his desk, he was shaking. Barb noticed it when he walked into the kitchen to get a drink of water.

"You okay, hon? You look a little tense."

"No, I'm fine. Just some complications with the Swenson case."

"Oh yeah. How's that going. Still think you'll get him a new trial?"

"Hope so. Just one or two more details."

Owen felt like he weighed five hundred pounds as he twisted the facts one more time. Barbara noticed and, when Owen set his empty water glass in the sink, she took his hand and lead him into the family room where she'd paused the TV for a commercial. They sat on the sofa. Barbara scootched closer to Owen and reached around to massage his shoulders. She could feel his tension; and after Owen gave a few satisfied groans, she began to stroke his hair. It was then she felt the wound on Owen's head. She rearranged his artful cover-up and saw the stitched gash.

"My God, Owen, this looks like more than a trunk closing on your head. What really happened here?"

Owen was about to describe again the closing of the trunk of his rental car on his head, adding that he was in a hurry and pulled the door closed with unnecessary force. But he couldn't speak. He hung his head.

"What's the problem, Owen?"

Owen's chin was almost touching his chest when he finally answered. "I didn't want to worry you, but this Swenson case took some scary turns when I was in Florida." He fingered his wound. "This was from a mugging."

"Really! Tell me about it."

Owen gained some composure as he told Barbara the full story. With each new element of the story, she slid further away and, lips pinched, squinted at him. She shook her head dejectedly when Owen got to the final piece about being blackmailed a few minutes before and his ambivalence at making the story public. When he finished, Barbara leaned back, crossed her arms and didn't say a thing for two full minutes before facing Owen.

"Well, Owen, I don't know what to say. I guess it wasn't till your last night in Florida that you could have felt in danger. And you came home the next day. But I think it was foolish sneaking around that lodge up in the mountains rather than coming home. And if you'd called me about your mugging, I would have inisited that you come straight home."

She sighed and gave a tight lipped "But that's water under the bridge. The real question now is what to do about that guy who just called you."

"Right. If It weren't for that call, I'd be feeling pretty good right now, with a decent shot at saving poor Charles Swenson."

Barbara leaned back and stared at the ceiling. After a wait that felt interminable to Owen but was actually only about thirty seconds, she turned back to Owen and said "I think you should just lie to him."

"And say what?"

"I don't think it makes any difference what you tell him because, until you gave the details to that guy Conry, you and Ranzone were the only players in the story who knew what was really going on. Ranzone's brother, the priest, had no idea what his big brother was really worried about. Same with that guy Zapatosky. Sure, they knew little Dougie had turned out to be a handful, but they had no reason to suspect what you and John Ranzone knew, or think you know.

"Your friend Pinkett and those two old men in Tampa know nothing about why you were really looking for Ranzone's brother. And, ta dah, the guy who mugged you and wants to blackmail you is still in the dark. It sounds like he doesn't even know Dougie is dead. Funny, how no one really sees the whole picture, like the kids in the kindergarden class who each get to feel one part of an elephant but can't imagine the whole animal. Frankly, even you and Ranzone are just guessing about Dougie being the Strangler. You could tell your mugger anything and he'd be hard put to know if it was true or not."

"That feels a little risky; but you're right, he's actually in the dark. Maybe I can work up a believable story."

Chapter 49

Because of his worry about the New Yorker, the next days passed very slowly for Owen, even though it did not take long for Peter Martin to report that Stuart had called and told him that, just maybe, he was wrong about Swenson and that knife. He probably was just cleaning his razor.

"Funny," Martin said, "but he didn't seem guilty or remorseful about being mistaken. All he said was he and his pals thought it was time to do right for Charles. Weird. Makes me feel terrible that I didn't cross examine him back at the trial."

Owen thought it was weird too. All he could think of was Arthur Marx and his theory of street based sentence commutations. Was that what was going on? And if it was, should he go along with it? God, this was getting complicated.

With less enthusiasm than Martin probably expected, Owen congratulated him and they spent a few minutes planning the details of the coming effort to get Swenson a new trial. Martin admitted that he no longer remembered many details of criminal law, much less the procedure for seeking a new trial on the basis of new evidence or recanted testimony such as would be the case with the Swenson appeal. Owen assured him that the Innocence Project would know the drill. That was their only business, after all.

When Owen reached Glassman with the news that Stuart had agreed to correct his testimony and Martin had agreed to take the case, Glassman was more excited than Owen had been after hearing those bits of news from Martin. And Glassman didn't register any suspicion about the motivation for Greg Stuart's change to his testimony. So Glassman readily agreed to meet with Owen and Peter Martin to educate them on the procedures for making the appeal.

They met at Glassman's office where Glassman gave Owen and Martin a brief tutorial on the Pennsylnavia Post Conviction Relief Act under which Swenson and Martin would have to make their appeal. That act applies to cases where the law has changed, new evidence obtained or defense counsel provided an ineffective defense. Glassman said, sardonically, with a wink at Martin, that their best grounds might be ineffective counsel, but that wouldn't work because such grounds must be claimed within one year after the defendant's sentence becomes final. Since the law hadn't changed, that left only new evidence as grounds for appeal, grounds that *would* apply since the new evidence they'd present was found more than a year after Swensons trial concluded. The new evidence would be essentially everything that Owen had uncovered plus the new testimony of Greg Stuart. They worked out a plan to involve Conry in a way that could help Swenson without putting Conry in the position of ratting on his friend.

Owen could not enjoy the apparent triumph in the Swenson case. First of all, he began to develop doubts about Stuart's promised new testimony. Perhaps Stuart and his buddies had just decided that, if Swenson was not the Strangler, then he had been jailed long enough. Of course, that didn't mean that Swenson was guilty. Owen had to remind himself that he'd considered Swenson innocent even before he had that last chat with Stuart. Who knows.

But more important now was the threat posed by that New Yorker who was going to call for an answer soon. The more he thought about it as he waited for his train home from the Market East station after his meeting with Glassman and Martin, the more he realized that the New Yorker had to know he was grasping for straws. His hunch about Ranzone was just a hunch, and if Owen refused to cooperate, the New Yorker would get nowhere with his attempts to make public his suspicions that Ranzone was murdered. Get nowhere except possibly create an ineffective disturbance that would upset no one but Conry and Ranzone's friends and family. And maybe expose Conry and him to suspicion.

He liked Barbara's idea about the big lie, or at least a big lie that would work its way around what he guessed the New Yorker already knew. Maybe Owen could take the position that there was indeed more to the Ranzone story and build the big lie from that premise. No more half-truths. Go all in with the big lie.

He called Geoff Shultz.

"Geoff? Owen here. Need to run something by you."

"Yeah thanks for finally calling. Sounds like there was no need to warn Conry with Ranzone kicking the bucket when he did. Right?"

"Not really. Just before he keeled over, Ranzone tried to shoot Conry. And me."

"No shit! Tell me about it."

Owen went into the blow by blow, including his pact with Conry and the complications of getting Swenson a new trial without involving Conry. He had no guilt about telling Geoff his pact with Conry. After all, Geoff had known about Ranzone long before that pact. When he finished the Ranzone part of the story, he paused. "But that's not the end of the story."

"Oh?"

"Yeah. Remember the guy who hit me on the head down in Miami? Well he called me trying to shake me down."

"For what? What's he thinking?"

"He guessed there was something going on with Ranzone, something more than his trying to prevent my writing an expose about a drunken brother."

"And?"

"He wants me to tell him what was going on. He thinks I was involved in something shady with Ranzone. He wanted $25,000 or he was going public."

"Public with what?"

"Well, his current theory is Ranzone was murdered by me or by other people up here who were part of whatever illegal enterprise Ransone was involved in."

Shultz said nothing but Owen could picture him shaking his head in disbelief.

"Wow, the guy's got some imagination."

"That he has. Between you and me, I wouldn't mind his going public. It would bring out the Ranzone story and force Conry to get involved."

"Why don't you tell him to do that?"

"I feel like I should honor my promise to Conry. If I have to break it I don't want it to be for the satisfaction of that New York sleaseball. And besides, we hope we can free Swenson without making the Ranzone story public."

"So what're you going to do?"

"Tell him a big, beautiful, believable lie. That's where I need your help."

"Gee, thanks Owen. You see me as an expert in fabricating falsehoods?"

"No, but you're always good at helping me think through things."

Shultz laughed. "Well I know you need help in the thinking area. So lets get started with that lie."

The two friends spent an enjoyable half hour concocting a believable story that incorporated what the New Yorker knew to be true, played with what they assumed he suspected to be true, and made up facts that he would probably accept as true. On his trainride home, Owen rehearsed the story until he bagan to believe it himself and when, a couple of evenings later, the New Yorker called, he felt ready.

"I've thought about what you said, whoever you are, and I want to stay out of this mess. But I really don't have anything particularly helpful and I certainly am not going to pay you any money." Owen cleared his throat. "But I will tell you the little I do know."

Shapiro snorted into the phone. "This better be good."

"Good, bad or indifferent, it's all I have to give. You decide."

"It all started when I was looking for something to work on for my sabba. . . . er, leave of absence from my university. I decided I wanted to look into the accuracy of police sketches drawn from witness descriptions. What I wanted to do was see how well they matched up with the real photos of the perpetrators when they were caught. I had in mind an experiment where my students would have maybe fifty sketches and fifty photos in front of them and be asked to pair them up. Get it so far?"

"Yup."

"Well, included in the sketches I got from police departmnents in the mid-Atlantic states were some without accompanying photos, meaning the perpetrators were never caught and photographed. One was of a suspect in an apparently random killing in 1991, in Baltimore, I think it was. No way I could use that one for my study.

"But about the time I received that sketch, I noticed a photo of a younger John Ranzone with his extended family: parents, siblings, children. He had a very distinctive looking brother, pointy ears, thin spikey hair and an overall look that he wasn't all there. To me, he looked like the guy in that unmatched sketch. I started making inquiries and found that the brother had, in fact, lived in Baltimore in 1991; but had relocated to Florida in 1992. No one in his family had been in touch with him for years. So I started hunting him down. I guess his big brother, John, heard about me and got worried. Maybe he too had some suspicions about his brother Doug. Who knows?

"From what I had learned about Douglas, he was such a marginal type of guy that, if he was that Baltimore killer, I might be able to get him to confess or at least agree to talk to authorities. So finding Doug became my research project. As you can guess, I was pretty sure I had tracked him down to the Bayshore section of Miami Beach, specifically a tiny park in which a lot of homeless hung out. But as you also know, not only was I not able to find the guy, but I was discouraged from continuing my search by you. So I came back to Philadelphia and I've started back on my original sketch/photo matching study.

"Now, if you want to make any money on this, the first thing you have to do is find Dougie. I have no interest in telling my story and, unless you have Dougie to interrogate, no one will believe the story if you tell it second hand. If I had a current photo of him, I'd send it to you; but all I had was a decades old family shot on faded newsprint and a crazy hunch. If John Ranzone hadn't apparently paid you to stop me, I wouldn't feel very strongly that my hunch about his brother being that Baltimore killer was correct. But if you find him, the Elect Ranzone Committee, or maybe the state Democratic Party, would pay you to keep it private."

"Well, Im not sure it's worth my time," said Shapiro "but maybe I can make this lemon into lemonade. Just don't you try and jump the gun and be the first with the news."

"Don't worry about that. I want out of this mess."

"Hope so" Shapiro mumbled before hanging up.

Owen felt good.

Chapter 50

The PA Act requires that appeals after convictions be brought before the judge who originally heard the case, if that judge was still active, or any other judge if the original trial judge had retired. The Swenson team couldn't decide whether or not it was a good thing that Judge Carol Angione, the trial judge, was still active. Just barely. She was phasing out her case load preparing to retire; and when Glassman called her to discuss the case, she was hesitant. Glassman argued that she at least had an obligation to hear their story and she agreed to a conference in her old chambers in City Hall. She had refused to move from them when the new Criminal Justice Center was opened across the street. Owen was invited to attend with Glassman and Martin.

Owen was a few minutes early for the conference. Judge Angione's chambers were on the top floor at City Hall. She shared an office with another older judge whose name Owen remembered from his father's days as a Philadelphia lawyer. Inside, a twenty something woman, dressed in a suit that looked like it hadn't been dry-cleaned and pressed in a while, greeted him and told him to take a seat in an area with walls of greying wood paneling that must have been quite elegant at one time. The waiting area was between the private offices of the two judges. He sat on a cracked leather bench and in a few minutes Glassman entered, looked suspiciously at the leather bench and stood waiting for Martin. When Martin arrived, the young woman in the suit led all three of them to a larger room where Judge Angione sat behind a huge walnut desk. The usual placques and photos of the judge with local pols and celebrities adorned the wall. A large American flag dangled on an eagle topped pole in the corner. The space reminded him of Kopinski's office, except for the huge desk and unpolished paneled walls. The judge didn't stand when they entered but waived them into the seats across her desk. Glassman introduced Owen and Martin, reminding the Judge that Martin had been Swenson's sttorney at the original trial and explaining that Owen had done most of the leg-work on the Swenson case. She spoke first to Martin.

"Mr. Martin, It's been a long time. I've had my clerk review the transcript of Mr. Swenson's trial and she seems to think you could have done better. All I really remember about the case was that it was difficult to keep the DA from prosecuting Swenson as the Kennsington Strangler even though he was never charged with any of those crimes."

Martin sagged a bit and exhaled slowly, then said "I agree with you that I could have done better. That's one reason why I'm taking on this appeal, and the new trial if we get one, on a pro bono basis. Hopefully I know my way around a courtroom better than I did when I was a pup."

The Judge smiled and seemed about to say something nice when Glassman spoke up. "And as far as the Kensington Strangler goes, we believe the DA's implication that our client was the Strangler was a significant factor in the case. We now know that he wasn't the Strangler."

Owen raised his hand to speak. "I've read the transcript your honor, and I was impressed with your fairness, your attempts to keep the Strangler matter out of the courtroom. I'm sure there were a lot of allusions to the stranglings by the prosecutor that were stricken from the record I read. But we still believe the DA poisoned the well, so to speak."

"Is that your grounds for appeal, Bob?" She raised an eyebrow to Glassman.

"No," Glassman said. "We have a recanted testimoney of one of the key witnesses against our client, and evidence that the DA did not share everything he should have with Mr. Martin. And a new witness who can challenge the statements of James Phelan, a key witness for the state at the original trial who, unfortunately, has since passed away."

"Hmm. Let me hear about it."

At this point Owen took the lead in their presentation, describing his conversation with Mrs. Phelan and his research about the Phillies game. Judge Angione interrupted at this point. "Your recanted testimony better be pretty good because what you've given me so far is pretty weak."

"I think it is pretty strong your honor. The witness who said he saw Swenson cleaning his knife now says he was just cleaning his razor. He's prepared to say just that at a new trial."

The judge said nothing for a while and they all sat in silence until she said "Tell me about the Strangler case. You say Swenson was not the Strangler. Why do you say that? I understand that he was never charged with those murders. But as I recall they ceased after he was arrested."

Glassman moved forward on his seat and said "That's correct, your honor. But we can build a strong case that the Strangler was someone else, someone who died several years ago. His crimes were covered up by someone in a position to do so. But that person is also dead."

"So, you want me to take you at your word that Swenson wasn't the Strangler. How convenient that the witness you are challenging and your new suspect are both dead."

"We also have a witness who can offer some convincing testimony that what we say is true. But that witness is hesitant to testify unless supoenaed."

Owen jumped in. "If you grant a new trial, we will subpoena him if you permit his testimony. His testimony is relevant to the Swenson murder case primarily because, as you've said, the Stranglings were the unspoken undercurrent to the original trial. Our belief is that, without that false undercurrent, had our new evidence and new testimony been presented at the original trial, Swenson would not have been convicted."

The judge sat back and crossed her arms over her chest. After a pause that was painful to sit through, she said "I'll take it under advisement and get back to you soon, Bob."

Three days after the conference with Judge Angione, Glassman called Owen with the news that the Judge would grant a new trial on one condition. A big condition: that the DA would have to hear the new evidence and indicate that, if a new trial were granted, his office would not prosecute Swenson a second time. Obviously, on the verge of retirement, she didn't want to open a high profile new murder case. Her condition would require another conference, this time with the new DA.

Conry agreed to meet with Owen at the same Broad Street coffee shop at which they had met a few days before. It took Owen a while to explain that, though there would be no retrial, it would probably be necessary for Conry to tell his story to the new DA in order to free Charles Swenson. Glassman and Martin doubted that the new DA would refrain from charging Swenson again, even with the new evidence, unless he heard the story of Ranzone's involvement. Conry disagreed.

"Listen Owen, if Swenson was innocent, it shouldn't take my testimony to convince anybody. He either did it or he didn't do it."

"Okay, fair enough. But don't you think a jury would have found reasonable doubt if they had heard all the correct evdence at the first trial, even if Ranzone had not forced in the suggestion that he was the Strangler?"

"Maybe. I don't know. But you'd find out with a new trial, wouldn't you?"

"But we won't get that new trial. The judge will only grant one if she's sure the DA will drop charges. And we don't think he'd do that without your testimony."

They sat in silence for a while before Owen said "This way you wouldn't have to tell your story in open court. Glassman thinks we could even get the DA to agree to keep your testimony confidential. The new DA's a great fan of John Ranzone and wouldn't want his reputation smeared any more than you do. If Doug Ranzone was still alive, maybe. Or if John were alive, sure. But they're both dead. So what has he got to lose by keeping secret everything you tell him?"

Conry looked like he was about to cry. Owen could feel for him. His hero brought down in front of the new DA, a new DA who had worshiped John almost as much as he had. Even if the telling of his story were kept secret, it would feel to him like a betrayal of his friend John. But he hung his head and in a whisper said "Okay. I'll do it."

Glassman's prediction was correct. The DA's hesitance to drop the charges disappeared after his confidential meeting with Owen and Conry. Though the story dumfounded him, he could see no reason why the two of them would make it up and, when Owen told him about the New Yorker making his blackmail threat, he shook his head. "I can't believe it. John was a hero of mine." He twisted his lips in thought. "But I guess, in the end, he had to be his brother's keeper. Tragic."

Chapter 51

It took several weeks before Swenson was released. Because he was still the Kennsington Strangler in the mind of the public, his release was preceeded with an announcement by the DA that the Strangler had been tracked to Florida where he died, apparently by suicide, two years prior. The announcement made very little splash in the media, so many years having passed since the Stranngler's crime spree. And Swenson's early morning release itself was not mentioned at all. There were no angry relatives protesting his release or looking for a lawyer to sue the City. Swenson was released with the $472 he'd had when arrested and he used some of that money to take a cab to his old Kennsington neighborhood, where he was shocked by the changes. He put money down for a small furnished room and spent the afternoon making inquiries in the few remaining eating places on the Avenue to see if any of them were looking for a dishwasher.

At about five, he walked down to Barkley's. The bar, at least, looked like he remembered it, although the clientele was older than it had been in his day. It took him a while to recognize that the older guys sitting around were his buddies from years back. He inched to a table in the rear with some barely recognizable faces, although he was almost certain one was Greg Stuart.

"Hey, guys. I'm Charles. Charles Swenson."

All four of the old men leaned back in their chairs and smiled. The one he thought was Greg Stuart said "Welcome back, Charles. I guess you know you owe us a big thank you. We figured you was in long enough and it was time for you to enjoy life a little. Have a seat."

EPILOGUE

Nearly two months had passed since the Swenson matter concluded and Owen had not written a thing worthy of a full professor on sabbatical from from a prestigious university. Not that he was required to, but he thought he should be able to show more for his time than an Innocence Project case he couldn't fully discuss. He several times thought of asking Glassman for a new case; and he even considered actually doing the police sketch study he had fabricated for that mugger from New York.

Finally, with only weeks to go in his leave, he began going to his office at the university each day about ten and writing a short story based on his Charles Swenson adventure. Names and places were necessarily changed; but the theme of the story was how difficult it could be to ascertain facts in complex situations, particularly with limited information. He could not get over the image of the kindergarteners puzzling over that elephant which Barb had used to describe the situation of the parties in the Swenson matter.

As a sophisticated university professor, however, he thought in terms of beliefs, hopes and overdriven strivings influencing perceptions. As a consequence, the characters in his story acted less from ideals and good or bad intentions and more from impulses they could not really detect in themselves. So, while the outline of the story was based on the real life events he had experienced, he spent considerable time on the motivation of the protagonist, the armchair detective. He suggested, sometimes quite openly, that his motives in taking on the case rested, not so much on a genuine belief that his unfortunate client was in fact innocent, but more on his own need to see himself as a savior of sorts. As a consequence, he added a scene toward the end of the story in which the Greg Stuart character was convinced by his friends at the old neighborhood bar to retract the critical but true testimony that had convicted their old drinking buddy. Bar-based sentence commutation.

He enjoyed describing the renamed characters in the story, capturing, as best he could, their appearance and their surroundings; except of course for the New Yawk mugger whom he had never actually seen. But he had no problem creating his personality: mean, violent, avaricious and without feelings for others. So it was with some guilty satisfaction that Owen read an article in the Florida news section of a discarded USA Today he found on his trainride home. The piece was about a former New York City cop who was beaten to death by a group of homeless persons in Caruso Park in the Bayshore district of Miami Beach. Apparently, the victim had been harassing the homeless population in the park for weeks about a missing person he had been attempting to track down.

The End

ACKNOWLEDGEMENTS

While *So Hard to Know* is the shortest of the Owen Delaney books, it took the longest to finish due to my own laziness and lack of energy and my inability to write an ending that I thought worked. It might never have been completed had it not been for Tim Wade and Libby Marx who read a late draft, sans ending, and stimulated ideas for how I should finish the book. That is not to discount the contributions of others, including Phillip Newey, Jeff Vorzimmer at Automat Press, and Bill McCarthy, all of whom noted that my original ending lacked punch. I am also indebted to Greg Hanson who, as always, was encouraging about an early version of the book; to Mike Schuessler who also read an early draft and corrected many details about the geogarphy of Kensington; to Brian Baxter for the description of the ideal Democratic gubernatorial candidate for Pennsylvania; to Craig Currie who helped me visualize the old Philadelphia City Hall courtrooms; to retired Philadelphia Homicide Detective Jim Dougherty who first described to me the phenomenon of street based sentence commutation; to Bernie Zimmerman whose final review gave me the confidence finally to write "the End"; and to Gerrie Materna Dames whose claims to being a born proofreader turned out to be true.

About the Author

Gene Caffrey is a retired Philadelphia lawyer and real estate investor who has had a life-long love of sports and reading. He has been married for 50 years and is the father of two grown children. His familiarity with the gritty streets of Philadelphia and his near total recall of its characters informs his writing with a refreshing authenticity. He now divides his time between Philadelphia, Sarasota and his farm in New Jersey.

This is his fifth novel in the Owen Delaney series, the four previous novels are *Shock Treatment, Two Souls, Sweet Caroline, and Finding Bridget.*

For more information on the Owen Delaney series visit:
www.owendelaneynovels.com, or;
www.facebook.com/OwenDelaneyMysteryNovels.

Made in the USA
Middletown, DE
29 June 2021